The School of Love

The School of Love

Short Stories by

Phyllis Barber

Phyllis Barber

To Lin -
May your
writing thrive
Best -

UNIVERSITY OF UTAH PRESS
SALT LAKE CITY
1990

LIBRARY OF CONGRESS CATALOGING-IN-PUBLICATION DATA

Barber, Phyllis, 1943-
The school of love: short stories / by Phyllis Barber.
p. cm.
ISBN 0-87480-337-3
I. Title.
PS3552.A59197S3 1990
813'.54--dc20 89-38861
CIP

The stories in this collection originally appeared in the following publications:

"Silver Dollars" in *Kenyon Review* (reprinted in *Neo*)

"Almost Magnificence" in *North American Review*

"Tangles" in *Fiction International*

"The Glider"—Honorable Mention, Utah Fine Arts Literary Competition—1985

"White on White" in *Cimarron Review* (reprinted in *Network*)

"Oh, Say, Can You See?" in *Utah Holiday*; also received First Prize in University of Utah Andy Adam's Prize for Short Fiction—1982

"Trees" in *Network* (*From the Attic*)

"Justice" in *Crosscurrents*; earlier nonfiction version published in *Utah Holiday* under the title "To Be a Hardened Criminal"; also received First Prize in Short Story Category, Utah Fine Arts Literary Competition, 1985; also a finalist in the *New Letters* Awards Series National Competition

"The Argument" in *North American Review*

"Baby Birds" in *Chariton Review*

"Anne at the Shore" in *Event* (Canadian)

An earlier version of this collection received Second Prize in the Utah Fine Arts Literary Competition in 1984 under the title *Great Basin Tales*

To my primary mentors in the school of love:
Geoffrey, Christopher, Jeremy, Bradley, and David Barber

And to my primary mentor in the school of writing:
François Camoin

God is love.

1 John, Chapter 4, Verse 8

Love is strange.

Sonny and Cher

Contents

The School of Love

Silver Dollars

''Las Vegas is a good place to live,'' says my dad behind the morning newspaper. ''Sunshine. And God's with us here.''

''But, Dad,'' I open a bobby pin with my front teeth and pin a stray wisp of hair into a nickel-sized circle, ''God's nice, but wouldn't you like to be something big? I mean, a zillionaire? Wouldn't you like a Cadillac like Mario drives?''

''Who needs Mario?''

''The insurance company you two work for,'' says Mama from the kitchen, a rolling pin in her hands, flour on the cutting board. ''Bet he makes Million Dollar Club again this year. Five in a row.''

''Six,'' my dad says as he closes his paper, stands to hitch up his trousers that have slipped under his paunch onto his slender hips.

''Good-bye, everybody,'' I say, stepping out the door.

I take a huge breath. Everything is alive outside, the night still happening. I hear the creaking rope of the trapeze lady at the Circus, Circus casino—the rope she climbs to get to her trapeze where she does tricks all night long. The wash of morning light over Sunrise Mountain never quite takes it away, all those sounds of music, the dealers' voices, the silver dollars.

The neighbor on the corner plays the flute at the Dunes. At night he puffs out his lower lip and blows across the mouthpiece of his long silver instrument. His deep magic notes still float over Bonita Avenue.

The neighbor across the street has green pebble grass and cactus trees. He owns Foxy's—the twenty-four-hour delicatessen on the Strip. When I sniff the early morning breeze, I smell his lox, bagels, and dills. I hear the sound of coins tumbling from his kosher slot machines, silver dollars falling out of the coin tray onto the floor, rolling across checkered tiles. The dollars roll into a heap under a small square table topped with a plastic basket of unfinished potato chips.

I love the night. I can feel it, even now while the sun shines over Sunrise Mountain, its rays piercing the sky and dividing it into pieces.

I'm going to be a showgirl soon, a terpsichorean like I read about in the *Las Vegas Review Journal.* In the daytime, I'll pose on high diving boards for the cameraman. I'll curve my derriere up toward the sky and act like I'm ready to dive. At night, I'll wear pasties and sequins and feathers, and Mother and Dad won't know. Besides, even if they surprised themselves one night and went out somewhere besides a church meeting, I'd be hidden in feathers, disguised with false eyelashes.

When I'm a showgirl, the flute player and the owner of Foxy's will read about me and start waving at me when they drive in and out of their carports. People will throw silver-dollar tips at my dancing feet. I'll bury them like seeds in our garden. When Mother goes digging for radishes, she'll find a treasure. I've got plans.

Sunday dinners, pot roast with stewed carrots, halved potatoes with browned edges, collapsed onions. Mother's farm cooking. We say Grace: "Heavenly Father, we thank thee for our many blessings. Please bless this food that it might nourish and strengthen our minds and bodies. May thy Spirit be with us this day, Amen."

Our seven pairs of elbows clash as we pass the bowls of steaming vegetables, green salad, and gravy.

"Shit, this is a brand-new tie!" says my dad when he spills some gravy.

"Vernon!" Mother glares like someone who is facing an army single-handedly. "You promised not to swear."

Sometimes, the real Vernon slips out, like the flick of a snake's tongue or the back side of his hand snapping against my cheek, but he's learned not to offend Mother, who makes his eggs just the way he likes them if he helps keep the peace.

He sits there on simmer and finally says, "I'm sorry." His apology is not a real one, though, just an exercise in manners. Maybe it's because his bones are small; they could snap and crumble like saltines, unlike Mother's, which are large and strong.

Dad coats a potato with gravy, swirls it around on his plate. "What did you learn in church today?" he asks me in a voice with fifty-pound weights on it.

"I think the new minister looks like Bat Masterson, even a loan shark." The minister wears a three-piece suit, has a moustache and slicked-back hair. He plays with the silver dollars in his pocket during his sermon.

"Watch your mouth," my mother says.

"You know," I say, "he reminds me a little of Mario."

"I wouldn't say that." Dad loosens his tie and asks my brother to pass the gravy again.

"Oh, I would," I say, tapping the edge of my water goblet with my spoon. "He moves like Mario."

"Would you listen to that girl talk?" my mother says. "What's happening to her, Vernon?"

"Could I please enjoy my potatoes and gravy?" he asks, his elbow on the table, his hand supporting his forehead.

On the way to my dad's office where I work after school, I detour through the Golden Nugget, act like I'm on my way to the ladies' room so I won't get asked to leave for being a minor. I see the white shirts of the dealers, their black neckties, their cuff links. I see them rubbing their well-manicured hands together, soft hands with squared-off fingernails like Mario's.

Bellied men in Hawaiian shirts and thongs push past me. They drop their cigarettes on the carpet and twist their shoe soles over the butts to crush them into flat, dead stubs. They walk hypnotized, like there's a dollar hanging on a fine line just beyond their outstretched fingers.

They don't see me. They don't see this future terpsichorean walking across the carpet, someone who will dazzle everyone's eyes with the silver dollars glued to her belly button, around her waist, hanging from her ears.

Someday, when I can get a stack of dollars high enough, they'll see. After I plant a treasure in my mother's garden, I'll build a tower out of the rest of my silver dollars. I'll pose in front of it in a silver lamé turban and five-inch heels.

* * *

When I arrive at the office, Mario is talking to Mrs. Benedict, the head secretary. Mario has curly black hair and a straight row of pearls for teeth. He wears a silver-dollar tie clip and riffles coins in his pockets. He reminds me of a flashing electric sign, the light reflecting from his gold cuff links, his wet teeth. He hums bits from Italian opera, and I can see Mrs. Benedict is not hiding her pleasure.

I slip past them into my father's office and slide behind a rickety typewriter table.

"Hi, Dad."

"Mrs. Benedict has so much to do," he is saying to the other two agents who share his office space. "Besides," he winks, "I'm teaching my daughter some secretarial skills in case some bounder leaves her high and dry some day."

Mario strolls down the hall and pokes his head into the room. "Hi, boys, how's it going?"

"You've met my daughter?" Dad says.

"Why, yes." Mario moves close to me in his perfectly pressed, European-cut pants. His hand is stretched out. "Your dad says you can type up a storm, sweetheart."

I lay my hand in his, smile, but feel uncomfortable with the way his teeth and eyes flash off and on like neon. I look down at Mario's tailored slacks instead, the slight bulge of silver dollars, the tiny seams around the zipper.

"Steamroll 'em, Vernon! With a daughter like this, you'll be in the Million Dollar Club in no time." He snaps his fingers and flashes out of the room. I can feel the night moving down the hall to the only door in the office with one name on it—*Mario Apoletti, Chartered Life Underwriter.* I listen to him, to the coins in his pocket.

I reach in to feel the dollar in my pocket. I run my fingernail over the little washboard grooves at the edge, then turn the coin in my palm. There's Miss Liberty's head under my thumb and the peace eagle's closed wings under my middle finger. I rub the capital letters—E PLURIBUS UNUM, PEACE, on one side, LIBERTY, IN GOD WE TRUST, on the other. The metal sticks to my fingers when I work it up to the tips and back down to the webbing where they join together.

* * *

Besides working in the daytime, Dad makes appointments with clients and leaves us at night. Sometimes I shiver while I wait, the wind penetrating the aluminum-encased panes. Sometimes I perspire in the heat. The wetness seeps through my curls and pulls them flat.

Dad comes through the door, a huge temper pressing against his skin. He yells at me to get to bed, then goes to his study, sits in his big chair, closes his eyes, shuts everything away from himself.

I tiptoe past his door, barely cracked open. I spy upon the sphinx and watch the light reflect off his forehead, watch his jaws work silently, correcting a flaw in a sales spiel, repeating the correction. I watch his arms fold across his stomach and his legs cross. I see his heart pumping, fluttering his ribs.

He turns grey as he sits there. Small grey hairs at the temples, wispy grey hairs in his nostrils. He sits there too long, until there are ashes in his face. Fingertips spreading ashes over his forehead, his cheeks, his chin. Ashes for my father, dropping from his face, flaking into piles where the silver dollars should be stacked.

Benny Binion might think he's God's gift to Las Vegas because he framed a million paper dollars under plastic at his Horseshoe Casino, but I could do better. I'd pave Fremont Street with silver dollars, Liberty heads, peace eagles, In God We Trusts, those audible dollars that clank into slot machines, ring in people's pockets, rub the warp and the weft of the fabric. Then everyone could walk on silver and sigh about the streets of heaven.

The Silver State—even license plates spread the word. Silver concho belts, silver hammered into squash blossoms. The silver runs through veins in countless abandoned mines, through my veins, too. I want silver around my neck, my wrist, my waist. I wish for a silver heart around my ankle or a silver disc on a long silver chain, engraved with peacock-feather swirls and my true love's name.

Silver. I will dot my sleeping eyes with silver dollars at night. The cool metal over my eyelids.

* * *

Late one afternoon, I watch my dad and Mario stand together in the hall, the sunlight from the window rippling the linoleum beneath their feet. My dad pulls up his pants again. His suit doesn't fit. I think he'd be more comfortable in loose Chinese silks, sliding the beads on an abacus, quoting Confucius. Instead, he stands there, pulling himself up as tall as he can, pulling up his pants, groping inside his jacket for the pens in his pocket clipped over a plastic protector.

I stand in the doorway of my father's small office and pretend to file my nails with the worn emery board. Can't have them break off on typewriter keys, an I or a P. I hang my head and cover my face with volumes of hair while my father talks like he doesn't care he's just heard about this year's winners for the Million Dollar Club.

"I've got my church," he tells Mario, "my family, my pie-making wife."

He brags he can go home to a pie every night. His wife, Zenna, can garden, preserve peaches, sew seams. His children are clean.

Dad struts in front of me, tries to tell a funny story to Mario, who doesn't bother to look out from under his velvet brows to notice my dad, dressed in ill-fitting slacks falling down around his heels. He jingles the dollars in his pocket while he tells the story about his friend, Jed, who had a belt buckle made with five silver dollars and a turquoise nugget. "He dared women to touch it. 'The gateway to my treasure,' he'd say."

Mario laughs, but not really. My dad looks around and sees me standing there. "That's my little Mary, you know."

I slide back into the office, sit at the typewriter, and type: *"Jingle your dollars, Dad. !@#$% *$$$$$$$$$."* I type all the white out of the page, trying to make night on the paper. I try to squeeze the light out of my eyes, but all I see is Daddy standing on fried pavement that curls the soles of his shoes. He tells jokes. No one listens. I grab his hand. "I'll buy you a float, okay?"

I reach for the dollar in my own pocket, feel for Miss Liberty, but the edge of the dollar has rubbed the threads raw in my pocket. The dimes go first. The pennies drop next, one by one. Before I know it, my silver dollar goes, too, slips big and clammy across my thigh. It hits the concrete and rolls away from me like the gingerbread boy who jumps off the cookie tray and hollers, "You can't catch me!"

I run like fire behind that dollar, sucking desert heat that burns my lungs and singes my tongue. Daddy runs behind me, running after the dollar, too. I can hear both of our lungs pound against our chests.

Suddenly, my dollar hits a crack in the sidewalk. It spins like a gyroscope. Then it slows, poises on its edge before it clatters onto the concrete. Sun glints off the engraving. The peace eagle spreads its wings, lifts off, and flies to the mountains, my dollar soaring in the sky. Daddy and I look at each other in disbelief. Our root-beer float!

''The pies will have to go,'' Mama said to my dad one day. ''It's because of the children. Our kids aren't going to have second best anymore.''

''Do what you have to do,'' he said, ''but don't forget my pies.''

''You know what Dr. Bascom said to me?'' she reports at the dinner table after her first day as an orthodontist's assistant. ''He said, 'We'll call you Zan instead of Zenna. That is, if you don't mind. Zan! That's got real class.' '' She laughs like she is fourteen. ''He looks like Mario, you know.''

She seats crooked-teeth adolescents in sculptured reclining chairs; she unfolds the paper towels and clamps them around necks with a beaded metal chain. The lady named Zan acts more exotic than the woman named Zenna. She walks like she owns something for the first time. She has lost a few of her farm-girl butter-and-cheese pounds, bought store clothes. The name Zan diminishes her strong arms and heavy bones; but even so, Vernon hopes he will find Zenna when he comes home at night.

''You're wasting away,'' he says. ''You're not home when you're home.''

Silver dollars in her pocket, the rolling pin at rest, Zan tells and retells stories about Dr. Bascom. She tosses in new phrases like ''vacation home'' and ''this year's Cadillac.'' Every night at the dinner table, she talks about the doctor's life as if it were a new fur coat. ''Dr. Bascom has his hands manicured like Mario. He puts a lot of money in the First National Bank of Nevada. I know,'' she says, ''I make out the deposit slips.''

Mama's crooked-teeth children file into the orthodontist's office to have silver-colored bands wrenched between their teeth. When Dad says he misses his pies, she points to our silvery mouths and smiles proudly.

I wish he could come home at nights with both pockets full of silver dollars. He'd be happy jingling them. They'd bounce off his right leg and my dad would smile and dance to the music they made. He'd lift his arms like a Latin dancer, ruffles on his sleeves, and he'd samba into the kitchen and flip coins into mother's pies. "Dollar pie tonight, Zenna. Forget our teeth. Forget our stomachs. It's Silver Dollar Pie Night. Riches for the rich. We eat dollar pie, we'll be the rich getting richer." Then he'd samba over my way and flip fifty dollars into the air for me to catch. I'd jump and rebound like a Globe Trotter. And we'd arm wrestle for dollars, play Tiddly-Winks with those big coins.

I wish he could clank into the house like a knight in a suit of silver instead of creaking past my door on the soft soles of old leather shoes, instead of turning his pockets inside out to empty the nickels and lint.

And I wish I hadn't had to ask him, but I was in need.

"Dad?"

He was washing his hands at the bathroom sink.

"I want one of those furry angora sweaters in a big way."

"So? . . ."

"Save me, Dad, I have to have one."

"You think you need to be saved?" He hung the blue towel back on the rack, walked into his study, and opened his filing cabinet. "Your mother knits. Ask her."

"Not like this, Dad. Besides, she works now."

He turns red in the face, then white. He turns into colors while I stand and watch. He's blue, then green in a way that makes me think he'll help me out this time. Then the pink rises around his collar. He swallows. "I can't."

"But you say that every time." I dig the toe of my pink flat into the carpet. I twist my foot around.

"Daddy, please. Everybody has one."

"If you say that again . . ."

I watch his guilt. He wants to say yes. Then I watch his anger. The colors are rising like the colors on a barber pole—turning, spiraling up and up, repeating themselves.

He takes three silver dollars out of his pocket. "I know this is nothing, but take it. And get more babysitting jobs."

I want to say thank you, but I say, "When are you ever going to make the Million Dollar Club? Wouldn't you just love to show everybody you're as good as Mario?"

I watch my father's colors fade. I feel his evaporation drifting away from me into that place where his face turns to ashes, where he is consumed. His eyes are turning backward into shade.

"Daddy, come back."

I quickly put the three silver dollars in his hand again and my arm on his shoulder. "Here, Dad. Keep jingling these dollars. Roll them in your hand. Rub them together."

He is changing to a transparent man. I can see inside his skin where his delicate bones join together at the hip, the ribs, and collar bone.

"Don't go away. Please stay here."

I bend onto my knees and start to kiss his hands, but the kissing is hurting my lips—those spiny bones that are cold.

"Daddy, come back. Please." I am watching a skeleton fold into a double twist and collapse against itself. "Papa," I plead. "I'm sorry I asked. I'll never ask again. Honest. I promise."

"These bones can only carry so much," he says.

When I nod my head yes, the skin begins to re-cover his femurs and tibias; hair resprouts on the new skin. My father re-forms in front of me—his balding scalp, the look of faraway places in his eyes, the small hips that can't keep a pair of slacks at his waist. He puts his hands out, palms up. I place my hands on his. "It isn't easy for me to say no to you, Mary, because I love you. It's just that there's only so much to go around."

"Well," I speak gently, "why does Mario have extra?"

"Mario is Mario. Different things matter to him."

"But why can't they matter to you? You'd like money. I know you would."

"I don't like the hard edges of people who have to have it," he says.

"But when you glitter, people see you. People want to be near you. They'll buy insurance from you then. Don't you understand?"

"Someday, you'll grow up, Mary."

On the Friday before Father's Day, I go to Ronzone's Department Store and ask the clerk to show me his best shirt. I have one month's worth of babysitting money in my pocket.

"Button cuffs or cuff links?" he asks.

"Cuff links, of course."

"White on white?"

"Like the dealers wear." I smile in anticipation, thinking how my dad will compare to Mario now.

When I get home with the box wrapped in a blue bow, I can't wait until Father's Day.

"Please, Dad. Please, I can't wait."

"I'd rather wait until Sunday," he says, lifting the lid.

"It was the best one in the store. White on white." He is still rustling tissue, still opening the gift.

"Do you love it, Daddy?"

"It's very nice, but this is too fancy for me."

"It's the most beautiful one at Ronzone's—the kind Mario wears. Cuff links, too."

"I hate cuff links. They get in my way."

He is folding white tissue over the folded shirt. He is closing the box and slipping the ribbon back over the corners and I don't know how to tell him he's making a mistake, that I've thought a lot about answers for him.

"Thanks, but just get me a plain shirt, okay?"

I take the box to my room, slip it under my bed, and listen to radio station KENO. I see floating pieces of my father's God-fearing forehead, freckled, tanned from the inescapable desert sun. I hear the smooth words he uses in his office, the swear words he forgets and uses around home sometimes. I feel his chameleon body sliding through my mind, the vertebrae of a lizard crawling and tracking my brain. And I hear Mario laughing down the office hall, feel his neon lights flashing with my pulse. I reach out to touch the wetness on his teeth, to touch his silver-dollar tie clasp, to circle my arms around his white-on-white shirt, to press my ear against his perfect tailoring.

And I start to breathe. A trainload of silver dollars is waiting just outside my window, the night is moving again, and Daddy, my daddy, fades into my night.

Almost Magnificence

She had been magnificent, almost. But now, trouble was, she leaked at the edges. Maybe somebody hadn't sewn the seams straight enough. God's sawdust doll, dripping flakes of sawdust.

For a while, concerned about the litter, God hired somebody to follow her around with a whisk broom, but that proved a full-time job and people had their own responsibilities. So God said, "Gee whiz, you'll have to take it from here, honey. I've got a lot to do. More dolls to make." So she just leaked around town, incrementally.

Trouble was, after a while, the leakage affected the order of things. Her husband couldn't sleep at nights for all the sawdust in the bed. He disappeared. Her child, allergic, sneezed too much and had to be asked to leave. Her brain slipped down to the esophagus, her heart sagged, and her uterus got stuck in a knee joint when it finally gave way to the termitelike excavation.

"Ma Ma," she cried like a Baby Cuddles. "Ma Ma." But her mother was gone, blown away like a crisp autumn leaf.

"Da Da," she cried, not like a Baby Cuddles, but sort of. But her father was gone, too.

So here was this almost magnificent lady walking around town, saying "Ma Ma" and "Da Da," and leaking. People felt sorry for her for a while. After all, she had been beautiful, and her mother had always dressed her in lace and Mary Janes. But when she started to wear banana-peel skirts, fresh cherry earrings and halved apricot pasties, and started to say "Whooo-ee," people shook their heads and wondered.

She thought about taking a job at the new health-food restaurant in town because her outfit would be appropriate for the lunch trade. But a hungry customer, not able to wait for his fruit salad with herbal dressing, might snitch one of her half apricots. With this in mind, she relapsed into her "Ma Ma" and "Da Da" routine and bolted the door.

Alone with her three cats, who liked her sawdust mixed in with their kitty litter, she dwindled down to a few powdery body parts, which her pets mistook for catnip.

Tangles

Alice sleeps with her teddy bears—grey, brown, and white, the natural colors.

The white bear has a sweet look in his beaded eyes and stitched mouth. His arms are stiff, and he is always reaching for Alice. He has a music box inside, so she sometimes sleeps on him as if he were a pillow. In between the musical phrases, she can hear the mechanics inside, the metal teeth plucking steel strings over and over, lullabye and good night.

The grey bear is dressed like a prince. A monocle. A royal blue satin sash over his chest. When she holds him, she thinks of waltzing in Vienna. Elegantly carved ceilings. Violins. Free-standing vases of fresh flowers.

The brown bear has tangled fur and moss-colored eyes. His snout is lifelike. Sometimes Alice hears him sniffing for food in the night. Once when she had eaten trout for dinner, this bear rooted under the covers, sniffing louder and louder. "No trout here," Alice had said, patting him on the head and scolding gently. She needed to sleep.

"Papa," Alice asked as she stood by him and his typewriter in her knee socks and penny loafers, "do you like me?"

"Of course," Her father rearranged the order of his stapler, three-hole punch, and tape dispenser and smiled pleasantly.

"How much?"

He put three pieces of paper in the typewriter and began to turn the platen knob. "About as much as anybody could like somebody."

Alice stood on one leg, like a stork, and hugged herself. "How much is that?"

"Alice, what do you want?" He flipped the paper release and lined up the edges of the bond, carbon, and onionskin. Then he began to type. He was very fast.

Alice started to hop on her one leg and flap her arms like a bird. She jumped up and down on the shag rug in her father's study. Her curls bounced in and out of their tight rolls, tangling slightly.

"That's enough, Alice," he said as he typed.

She kept hopping.

"I'm warning you." He had arrived at the second paragraph already.

Alice stopped and stood on both legs. She put her hands over the typewriter keys.

"Type on me, Daddy. 'Now is the time for all good men' . . . like I'm learning at school."

He swiveled away from her and reached into the bottom drawer of his filing cabinet. "When are you going to grow up?" He handed her a pad of paper and fished for a ballpoint pen in his caddy keeper for pencils and pens. "Draw a picture while I type."

Alice sat down where she had stood, half on the carpet, half on the sheet of hard plastic that made it possible for her father's chair to roll around wherever he wanted. She took the top from the pen, screwed it onto the blunt end, and began to draw circles—lopsided, oval, tangential. Circles within circles, bubbles, suds. The yellow pad was soon covered with circles that grew bigger as the pen dug deeper into the paper, deep enough to leave impressions on at least three more pages.

Alice's hair winds down to her waist. It's like gold. Curls, bounteous hair that bounces when she moves and looks as if it rolled out of a silk factory, worms spinning for days on end.

Sometimes when she walks from school, a man walks behind her, wanting to put his fingers inside those curls, to twist the spray of gold around his fingers, to lift the tresses to his lips, kiss the gold, make a moustache, a wig, a trousseau for himself. He'll tie the hair around her wrists and braid it into a cord, which he could use to lead her away.

She turns to see his face. It is old. She sees yellow in his eyes—the eggs of the eyes yolky with streaks of blood fringing the pupils. She laughs at him, the one who trips on her heels and reaches for her golden hair.

* * *

After he saw her walking across the room in high heels for the first time, her papa said, "Alice, you listening to me?"

"Of course, Papa."

He paused. "Alice, about men . . ."

"Yes?" She knelt on the shag carpet, wound a strand of hair around her finger, and leaned on the arm of his reclining chair.

"How do I say this?"

"What, Papa?"

"They only want one thing."

Alice looked up at him with her big blue eyes. He had blue ones, too, and was rubbing above them with his handkerchief.

"You shouldn't wear that two-piece outfit," he said. "Your midriff shows."

"My midriff? That's a funny word."

"It's the softest part of a female."

Alice decided to get him a drink of water. She hoped that he wouldn't start quoting Norman Vincent Peale or the Bible.

"Papa," she said, letting her hair fall in a tangle and pushing her eyeglasses tight to the bridge of her nose, "you just worry too much. Men don't make passes at girls who wear glasses."

He pushed the lie-back button on his recliner and stared at the ceiling.

Alice kissed his balding head where a wrinkle was beaded with light oil. "I love you."

In the store's dressing room, Alice finishes poking the laces through the grommets. She looks down at the two fleshy bubbles at the top of the corset and laughs for joy. An ice-cream soda.

"Today's the day the teddy bears have their picnic," she sings to her reflection in the mirror.

The corset is red satin with black lace. When it had hung on the sales rack, Alice had stretched its garters like they were slingshots and flipped the other corsets.

"He'll love it," the saleslady had confided.

"Who's he?" Alice asked.

"With this on, honey," the saleslady put both of her hands out in front of her, flat palms like a traffic cop, "they'll come in droves. Trust me."

Alice had stepped into the dressing room, carefully folded her knee socks inside of her loafers, hung her dress on the hook, and worked for thirty minutes to get the laces tight in the right places.

For the third time, the saleslady rips the curtain open. The sliding drapery hooks squeak over the rod. "What have you decided?" she asks, chewing Doublemint behind tight lips.

"I'll be right out," says Alice.

She wiggles into her knee socks and slips back into her loafers. She folds her dress and her half slip over her arm. Putting her glasses on again, she pays the saleslady and walks out into the sunshine.

The man with yellowed eyes drives by in a foreign car. He steps on his brakes and cranes his neck toward Alice. She smiles, curtsies, tosses her hair and walks away, the unattached garters slapping gently against her thighs.

"Papa," said Alice, "I'm leaving now. It's time." She was dressed in a houndstooth-check traveling suit and a white pillbox hat, and she carried a white patent-leather bag that matched her shoes. The Indian-summer grass in the vacant lot next door looked like wheat, silky and thick at the tips.

He rested his hand on her shoulder and patted her briefly. "You're my big girl now."

She smiled at him with Revlon-red lips and well-lined eyelids. Her eyebrows had been brushed up and her lashes separated from their mascaraed tangles with a straight pin. A furry look to her blue eyes.

"I can only give you love that lasts forever," Johnny Mathis was singing on the hi-fi through the open window. Alice's brother stood in the yard peering through a magnifying glass, his whole face transformed into the All-Seeing Eye. Her mother stood in the doorway licking the back of a wooden spoon. "Don't forget to write," she called.

Alice raised her eyes to her father's and saw her head with its pillbox hat reflected in the pupil of his eye. She wondered if he looked that small in her pupils, too.

"Remember what I've taught you," her father said, adjusting his tie. "And watch out for all those men."

A silver Pontiac pulled up in front and the driver honked while Johnny Mathis was winding up with "That's all," in the living room.

Alice picked up her cosmetic case and teddy bears and blew a kiss to her mother and brother. Her eyes swept the tips of her father's shoes as she pivoted toward the car door.

Alice joined the circus. She got a job riding elephants in an electric-pink sequined tutu. Between rehearsals, she played Canasta with the freaks, their crowd the only accessible one, since the aerialists and ballerinas snubbed newcomers.

The Dwarf had been the one to see her walking down the fairway. He often stood at the opening of his striped tent, staring at the ballerinas bouréeing by who never stared back. One day he spied Alice tripping along in her flip-flops.

"Canasta?" he asked. She stopped to shade her eyes from the sun and see who spoke.

"Pinochle, too," she said.

They shuffled cards together that very day. The World's Biggest Lady joined them. She wore eyelashes made from real mink and strawberry-colored lipstick painted in peaks. She sat on three folding chairs tied together with nylon rope, ate chocolate-covered pears, and held her cards in a perfect fan shape, which she used to cool herself when the tent got stuffy.

The Dwarf perched high on a bar stool. He had nubbed digits and, therefore, trouble holding his cards. Alice offered to hold them for him and promised that she wouldn't peek. But when his hands were freed from jacks and aces, they started to wander along Alice's thighs, kneading and squeezing with what dexterity he could manage.

"Your paws are bigger than kindness," she said, unable to push them away because of the cards she held.

"I like sensitive women," he whispered to Alice while the World's Biggest Lady went to the refrigerator for more pears. He reached past her buttons and under her skirt.

"But it's your turn," she said, her eyes wide and blue and searching for the World's Biggest Lady to reappear in the doorway.

"I'm taking it." His nubs tweaked the curly hair between her legs.

Alice smelled the chocolate first, then the pears, before she heard the World's Biggest Lady's jewelry jangle.

The Dwarf folded his paws, Sunday-school style, across his broad belly that seemed to puff out right then and there.

Alice moves into an apartment. When she goes shopping at the mall, she carries an umbrella with a bamboo handle. She hears breathing behind her and turns to check.

It is the man with yolky eyes. Those eyes are trapped in the shift between his upper and lower bifocal lenses—two giant, weepy eyes. Water in those eyes as he walks under the greenhouse canopy at the shopping mall, his brown felt hat dough in his hands.

"Respect for the man," he mumbles to Alice as she starts to walk faster, her shoes slapping her heels.

"Respect for the man," he starts to scream when she pays no attention, his eyes sudden Chinese slits of rage, his face rose red. He screams until all the shoppers bow to the ground to cover their ears with their elbows, just as in Khan's ancient court.

"Where is she?" He walks across the people, looking for Alice, one foot in the small of every back. The flower seller who has a gazebo in the middle of the mall hides behind the counter as the man sweeps six vases of gardenias into a wicker basket. The tipped vases spill water through the loosely woven basket onto his light brown shoes. He begins to toss gardenias, smiling broadly as a western sky.

"Flowers, my children," he says in a changed voice. "Sniff them. Know that you are flowers, too—delicate petals. Where is she?"

The people stay curled into their knees as the man treads over them again, though a few sneak their fingers out to grab gardenias. Suddenly, the man sees a hand wrapped around bamboo. He bends over Alice as she tries to burrow into the linoleum floor.

"A flower," he whispers and bends lower. "Fairer than all others." His lips press into her forehead. "Love one another," he says, kneeling by her side, taking her hand, and lifting her up. "Be not afraid."

Heads begin to rise as after a dust storm. People rub their eyes and pick up the remaining gardenias, maybe to take home to sniff or to press in a heavy book as a memento of this occasion.

She sleeps restlessly, turning over and over. Her hair looks frightened. It stands erect on one side as if it had an electric charge buzzing through it.

Her placid teddy bears surround her with predictable expressions. Their plastic eyes stare into the night, no worry in them as Alice wrestles with her pillow and gathers the bedsheets into knots in her hand.

"Papa," she calls out. "Don't." He is pushing her into a treasure chest full of bears. Alice starts to toss her own teddy bears onto the floor and into corners. Her hair has turned wet and stringy, the electrical current inert.

"Papa," Alice moans through her teeth. "Don't lock me in there. Can't you hear them roaring and gnashing their teeth?"

Suddenly, Alice sits up in her sleep and begins to stroke her father's head that rests in her lap. She strokes his neck, his shoulders. He is stuffed like her bears, and his arms reach out stiffly from his sides. As her fingers feel the braille of matted hair on his chest, the tangles of hair, she sees a key stuck into his ribs. She twists it. "I love you most of all," the mechanical voice says from deep inside.

She touches his hard plastic eyes and straightens the sparse hair on his shiny head. Then she sinks back under the bedcovers into sleep.

George walked up to Alice on a sunny day. He looked her straight in the eyes and told her that she was the most beautiful woman he had ever seen and he had to have lunch with her.

They ate at an outdoor cafe, Louisiana style. She cracked her crawfish into halves, picked at bits of flesh, and discarded translucent legs and hulls while commenting on the molasses muffins with the chewy texture. He raved about the sauce on his blackened redfish until a piece of pecan caught in one of his teeth. He had to ask for a toothpick.

"Teeth are a bother," she said. "Always have to floss or brush or water pick."

"How many lovers?" he interrupted. "You have that look about you."

"What look?"

"I can't quite explain."

"Try." She buttered another muffin.

Alice has a piano. Not a harpsichord or an electric organ, but a piano that sits in her living room, all big and black on three legs. It has pedals, her piano with white keys and black keys and cracks between. It is her friend and consort. With her teddy bears beside her, she sits on the bench perspiring, her legs apart, her feet pedaling and pedaling until her piano starts to roll away as if it were a bicycle. The wooden floor creaks and trembles with the weight. And then they come to the door, and the big black piano is wider than the frame. But as the crescendos grow louder, the door frames don't matter as she pedals her way out of the house, driving her piano through bricks and paneled windows. They drive down the street, the small casters rattling over the scattered rocks. Alice singing, "Hold me, piano. Be mine, bears."

One night before bed, Alice put on a mask to go to the Viennese ball with her prince bear. She wore a regal blue silk gown, fancy at the neck and hemline. Sweeping into the ballroom, she looked left and right to see if she knew anyone there. Her father was hovering over the buffet table, sipping champagne and nibbling on a chocolate-dipped strawberry.

Alice minced across the floor in her see-through shoes and the prince bear turned his mechanical head left and right until Alice had to rewind him behind a potted plant where no one would notice. Offering her companion a cashew from a silver dish, Alice finally ate it herself, but not before she noticed the man with yolk-colored eyes standing under an archway with two officers of the guard, George leaning against a marble column, and the Dwarf sitting at a card table playing Canasta with the dowager queen.

"Let's dance," she said to the prince bear, who was looking especially elegant and courtly. She held him close to her and buried her head in his shoulder while they turned to three-quarter time, Alice lifting him just high enough from the ground. She and the bear turned until the room began to whir past them with its bright colors and faces blurring—Papa, the Dwarf, George, and the man with the eyes.

"Dance with me, bear. Dance with me."

The music distorted as they turned faster, the three-quarter time losing its crispness, and suddenly they both rose from the ground, whirring and looking down on everyone's heads. A blur. Alice's ball mask began to pinch her face as the centrifugal force grew stronger. Ripping it off, she threw it at the man. One of the officers snapped his head up in her direction and yelled that she better come down right that minute. The prince bear and Alice, floating and turning above the silk, the diamonds, the polite smiles and the four men.

"No," said Alice to the officer. "No."

He grabbed a long hook that was used ordinarily to open high windows. He tried to hook one of her ankles to bring her down, but she turned too fast, horizontal to the parqueted floor, Alice and the bear, a Casablanca fan on high speed.

The women in ball gowns started to complain that their hair was getting mussed with the draft; the fringe on the crown prince's epaulets was tangling; the orchestra's sheet music was flying around the room.

"Alice," she heard her papa calling. "Alice, come back. I want to tell you something."

"What, Papa?" She kept turning.

"Alice, I need to talk to you."

"About what, Papa?"

"About men, Alice."

"You already told me about them."

"It's important." He shifted his champagne glass to his left hand. "Come here."

Obedient, Alice slowed and sank to the floor, straightened the silk ruffle over her shoulder, and walked over to her papa, who had just finished laying a fiver across the officer's palm to soothe his pride.

"Alice, my dear." His eyes shone, smooth with champagne, as he put his hand on the ruffles on her shoulder. "It's like this."

"Like what?"

"Somebody, possibly your mother and I, made you very beautiful. It's time for you to get a husband and stop dancing with bears."

"But, Papa, I like their company. They don't want anything."

"Alice," he sighed and shook his head, "there's no future in bears."

She looked up from the black tie at his neck, straight into his eyes. "What is my future, Papa?" She began to sway to Strauss's "Artist's Life" that had just begun to play in the background. Alice's father took her by the waist and led her onto the parquet floor. They kept perfect rhythm together, her father light on his feet.

"You dance much better than the bear," Alice told him. Their cheeks brushed together in the crowd of dancers.

He squeezed his fingertips into her shoulders, then released them. "Alice, my dear, what can I tell you?" He looked up at the thousand drops of light in the chandelier above the pattern of their waltz.

"Tell me the truth, Papa."

She saw a myriad of tiny waltzers and her own blue silk ruffles against cream skin reflected in her father's eyes.

The Glider

It was back. Just as she spoke louder than she should into the telephone, "Harold, I need it today," accentuating every syllable so he'd understand, she saw the glider sail across her window frame. The sight was a momentary relief from Harold telling her he had a backlog of orders six miles long.

"But you've got to come!" The telephone cord wrapped around her legs as she listened and paced. She stabbed the note pad with the point of her pencil, gouging black-rimmed holes into the paper, and then she stomped the slat on the rocking chair with one foot until it rocked furiously.

"Harold," she repeated, "I need the heifer today. T-O-D-A-Y. You know I've waited almost too long to get her bred. Stop giving me the runaround."

She raked her fingers through her hair and pulled it to feel sensation at the roots. She was alive, and Harold was trying to tell her she didn't matter out here at the end of the unpaved portion of the county road that wound through insignificant clumps of hills. Harold who couldn't see past his bent-sausage nose. Harold whose buttocks snapped when he walked, rolled to each side and bristled with arrogance. Harold who'd always called her "Cow Bones."

As she listened to him ranting on, her hand folded and unfolded angrily at her side. She kicked the door jamb, wishing it were Harold's shin, wishing she could budge him from his self-satisfied notion that the world turned for him and his truck with the row of amber lights across the top.

When she hung up the phone, she heard his bull laugh reverberating in her ears. "Of course, old girl," he'd said. "At noon, maybe, unless Lover Boy Harold gets seduced on the way."

"Damn that Harold. Ignorant hunk of flesh. His arms look like two shanks of beef."

The remnants of their conversation ran through her head like water through an antique drain. Martha pulled her whittling knife from its homemade leather sheath, a project she'd made in her high-school shop class where she'd first encountered Harold Lund, and started to hone the edge. Trying to calm herself, she concentrated on the real sounds in the room—the clock's swinging pendulum, the knife against the leather strop—and thought of the glider drifting somewhere in the sunlight. It would be back.

Besides the ranch her father had passed on to her when he was dismissed from the school of life on Highway 89, he'd passed on broad shoulders, lanky bones, and a sense that people should strive for perfection. As she sharpened the knife, her movement had a hint of old hinges, her long bones loosely connected, but her mind seemed to demand a tighter precision than her appearance suggested.

When she was satisfied with the absolute sharpness of the knife's edge, she slid it back into the worn leather casing and sank into the rocking chair, stretched, dropped her head against the headpiece, and filled herself with fresh oxygen. The glider's crystalline whiteness reappeared in the sharp blue spring sky. It floated like a hawk on the currents and seemed oblivious to the goings-on in terra firma. And then it floated out of the frame of her picture window as it always did.

She glanced longingly at the puzzle on the card table—a half-finished crazy quilt with paisleys, taffetas, and grosgrain ribbons. It tempted her—the elusive pieces waiting to be found, the luxury of avoiding the work that must be done to prevent the ranch from being choked to death by grass and weeds. Her record player tempted her, too. A Brahms intermezzo, perhaps. Or Ralph Vaughan Williams. Something soothing in this cheese-grater world that was shredding her little by little. Broken fences. Hoof-and-mouth. Last year's drought. But the glider was out there.

"Time to move," she muttered to herself. She shuffled in her untied boots past the card table, across the pine floor, the two braided rugs, and extracted a new pair of shoelaces from a brown paper sack. Bending over to thread careful X's through the grommet holes, each X with the right-hand lace on top, she felt Papa in her thoughts again . . . Papa in his faded denims, not in too big a hurry, just taking his time, making X's the same way. She stroked his old leather bag before she tugged it from under the window seat and hoisted it over her shoulder. *I'll keep my promise, Papa. I'm doing my best.*

Outside, Martha felt wet chill mixed with hot morning sun and noticed a chalk smudge of moon on the western horizon. She shaded her eyes. New green sprouted everywhere, even through the tepee mounds of last year's dead grass. The upper field would be dry enough to plant alfalfa this afternoon, but first she needed to fix the fence, just in case Harold kept his promise to bring the heifer by noon. Too good a pedigree to mix with the herd. She'd been waiting two years to afford her, had made arrangements a month ago to get her bred, and Harold kept stalling and driving her crazy. That cocky calf roper on the two-bit rodeo circuit who never said excuse me when he belched and who thought all the women in the state curled their hair in the morning just in case he might drop by.

She stepped on flagstones across her front-yard patch of cultivated grass, then into quagmire, her heels squishing in and out of each step until she stopped, her mouth open, and looked up.

There it was . . . her white glider, glossy smooth. The same one that had been flying over her field off and on for the past two springtimes, ever since her father's accident. The glider was a good omen. A floating promise. It caught a current and dipped and turned on invisible waves of air. It arced and languished over her field before it rose above the ridge, banked to the right, spiraled downward, and rose again. A flurry of seagulls, like scattered pieces of torn paper, circled the tail of the glider before it disappeared, but she knew it would be back. When she willed it to come back it always did, as if maybe she had extrasensory connections with the white beauty that sailed into her life with the springtime.

Now, instead of plodding through the mud, Martha leapt from edge to edge of each puddle. She hopped her way across the lower field and through the stick-like spines of last year's weeds. They jabbed her legs and scratched white streaks across her blue denim, but she didn't care as much now that the glider was back.

The wire fence sagged low to the ground between fence posts. Martha slipped the pouch from her shoulder, hung it on a cedar post, and dug for some double-prong staples. She found almost everything else—finishing nails, roofing nails, lag screws—but had to dig hard for the staples. What a mess, Papa would have said. He loved precision. He used to run his fingers over smooth joinings on a cabinet face and talk about people who cared enough for the slow, exact way of doing things.

Enough staples found, she yanked the cold stiff fence wire and threaded the hammer handle into the crushed angles. As she twisted, the angles yielded back to their original L-shape. The sound of her hammer echoed, solitary, as she tapped the staples into wood. But her repairs didn't look quite right. Slightly askew, they wouldn't stay repaired for long.

And then it came back, just as she'd willed it to. Quiet—unlike the jets from the air base that sometimes roared over her field, leaving a white snake cloud in their wake. The glider hovered and then eased across Martha's sky. "Perfection," she whispered. She waved as she used to at railroad engineers who leaned out of yellow diesel engines and touched the brims of their striped caps in return, but there was no response from the glider that slithered through the sky and out of sight. Maybe there was no pilot. Maybe the whole thing was a gift just for Martha. A disguised messenger from the gods. Hermes. Mercury. Even Jesus. The white that shimmered while Martha contemplated the possibility of pure essence.

Martha looked down at her feet rolled onto their edges in the uneven field. The abrupt overturnings of soil reminded her of Harold, who was so gross. *Acts like he's God's gift to women. Square head set on a square neck like stacked cinder blocks, still thinks he's the main attraction in Milburn at age forty-one.*

She'd seen him at the hardware store last October, walking the aisle, wearing his usual Stetson with the hawk feather in the brim.

"How're things?" he'd said.

Martha dug her finger into the profusion of three-penny nails and stirred them as if they were thick liquid.

"You been doin' pretty well since your dad . . ." He picked up a paper bag and shoveled it full of finish nails. "Course, you always thought you could carry everything around by yourself with those cow bones of yours."

"So, how's Glenda?" Martha asked, a slight twitch of triumph in her set mouth. "I hear you finally got a new truck."

She'd heard about Harold's wife. How she'd driven his green Dodge truck through Milburn screaming all the way, "Shithead! Shithead!" Glenda rolled down the windows and yelled at everybody she saw in front of the Mercantile and the Texaco gas pumps.

"Harold Lund is a shithead. You tell him for me." Nobody had seen her or the green truck since except for Mett Larson. He said he'd seen her and the truck in front of the Sundowner Lounge with another man and with her newly bleached hair curled in tight springs.

Harold brushed past Martha on his way to the counter. She heard the coins jingling in his pocket. Even though she'd sucked in her stomach and chest, he brushed against her anyway and didn't say excuse me. " 'Bye, old girl," he said.

Martha worked her way along the fence line trying to envision Papa on the front porch, Papa after work hours, looking bare without his Stetson, sharpening his knife on the strop and telling Martha about each piece of wood having something of its own to say if the whittler is sensitive. Papa, always talking about the heart of things—chunks of wood, bits of coal in the fire, even the gentle sounds a man's heart will make when he's not pretending to bigness. "Takes a big heart to live small and contented."

He'd been teaching her to whittle a penny whistle, how to angle the knife for hollowing.

"Take you, Martha," he said, sniffing the pine sap stuck on the edge of his knife. "Not many men content enough to see you're some fine girl. Strong. Hearty. Lucky man with eyes to see you."

Remembering the smell of pine, Martha tapped a weathered post with her hammer. The wood didn't buzz. Solid enough for another season, and she smiled with the thought of his weathered eyes. Her papa. The only real gentleman she'd ever known and a far cry from the likes of Harold Lund, even though he never could match yield with the Lund operation.

When the glider flew overhead, the sun and the fresh air breezed through her body, their cleanliness lifting her to a heady giddiness. And Martha could feel the freshness that filled her veins and made her know, once again, about real beauty. Purity that united a tiny human with the column of light from the place above the sun. Real music in the sky like the sound of a violin following an ascending bird. All an immense contrast to the memory of herself and Harold digging postholes last spring to fence new pasture for the extra stock she'd bought from him. She'd been leaning in close to check the depth of the hole before shimmying the post down in, and her breast pressed against his arm. He looked straight at her chest.

"Martha has tits," he said. "Hey, everybody," he spooled his hands into a megaphone and yelled to the empty air, "Old Cow Bone's got tits on her."

Martha kicked him in the shins. "You ignoramus. You don't know the first thing about anything."

"I'm supposed to treat you like a lady?" He laughed.

"What do you know?" She stuck her shovel hard into the pile of dirt they'd dug.

"That you're horny. Horny for me."

"You don't know squat."

"Ain't nobody around here gets to you, Martha, except me. I'm the only man big enough to take you on." He cupped both hands over her breasts and pressed his blunt lips into her face like a bowling ball into tenpins. "You'd like me to take you right now, too. Throw you down on that pasture grass and rip off your overalls. You know you want it. You know."

And Martha ran. She ran like a powerful quarter horse, determined to find a place where she could breathe, lie back on the ground, and stare up at the big sky.

When Martha went inside to check the time—1:45, long past Harold's promise—she bent over the card table and plucked a five-nubbed piece from the loose puzzle pieces. She held it up to the light from the picture window and turned it in her hand. *Looks like a melted star. No,* she smiled, *looks like Papa. No hat, but a head, two arms, and bowed legs.* She rotated the cardboard in her fingers like a cartwheel.

At that same moment, in the backdrop of blue sky behind the cardboard piece, the glider slid into the window frame, stopping just above the puzzle piece as if waiting for Martha to come outside again.

Suspended, stark still, it hung like a jewel on a pendant. Martha held her breath as if to capture the quintessential bird forever in that moment, hovering, graceful, its white outline scintillating in juxtaposition to deep blue. While Martha held back the exhalation that would disturb this absolute balance, the glider suddenly cut a sharp right angle from its place in the sky. It dove into the ocean of blue. It followed its nose along a perfect plumb line, spinning as it fell, dropping faster and faster until it rammed into the field, its nose burrowing into the ground. Tail up, the glider teetered as if deciding which way to fall, indecisive before it flopped onto its belly. Violent fingers of mud splashed over its sides as it lurched and then rocked from side to side, nestling into the field, making its own bed where Martha usually plowed.

She pressed the cardboard piece hard against her palm, held her breath again, squeezed her eyes shut. "No," she said. Then she shouted the word.

The pressure of the cardboard cut the shape of a melted star and a hatless man in Martha's hand. "Papa. No." Her head shook miniature noes as if a thousand of them could change something, and then she stopped and opened her eyes. The clock's pendulum was swaying. The leather pouch was hanging on the coat hook, still full of staples, her hammer, nails, and screws.

The picture window enlarged with blue and sunshine, hardened waves of sloughed earth, pools of stagnant water, and a crippled bird sprawled across her field. Through the glass, Martha's usual world shrank to toothpick telephone poles threaded with single-strand, four-ply thread from a spool, and spider-woven ribbons of road. No familiar sights to comfort her.

Her rhythm shifted to slow motion as she walked toward the door, grabbed for the tool pouch, and slipped back into her boots. The spiral cord on the telephone was cramped with too much twisting and hung in a tight tangle. *The telephone.* Martha lifted it from its cradle and dialed each number as if it were an extension of her finger. *Maybe Harold will answer.* She listened to the busy signal, a ramming fist of sound that disregarded Martha standing there, her tears running into the mouthpiece and filling the round black holes. *The kitchen chair. Sit in it. Tie your shoes.* The pouch slid down her arm and interfered with her intentions. She tied an awkward bow, doubled it, and pointed her feet at the door. The telephone again. Busy signal. *Walk through the door, through the screen, to the field.*

Mud sloshed over the top of Martha's boots onto her socks and inside her boots. She looked for goldenrod that might be blooming in the field. She saw the glider and then she didn't see it because she wanted someone to wave to her to tell her to look at the goldenrod. But all she saw were two gigantic wings spread across eight rows of alfalfa. Green leaves, three in a cluster. Purple flowers.

And then, the glider was under her hand. She rubbed the wing's edge. Smooth, satin smooth. "Someone loved this piece of work," Papa would have said. "Smooth as a baby's skin." She shielded her eyes from the glare on the canopy, blinded to the interior, and stroked the place where the canopy melded into the body. Too much mud. Her knife. Her pocket, her hand groping for the sheath, slipping the knife out of its case.

The plane sat low on its belly. Martha cleared the mud from the breast-high canopy, scraped the plastic with her knife edge, and rubbed the traces away with the sleeve of her light wool shirt. She bent into the reflection with both hands cupped at the sides of her eyes.

There was one man. He was still. His eyes were closed, his hands hanging down, fingertips folded against the floor. He wore a leather flight helmet strapped under his chin. Minuscule seams of red scored his cheeks, jagging toward his ears, suddenly changing direction, up to the temples, over the eyes. His face was split into a thousand pieces. He wore brown eyebrows and a strong, aristocratic nose. Thin lips. His face was split like her crazy-quilt puzzle, yet no piece was missing. He was all there except for a voice.

Martha turned to see if Papa might be behind her, holding a stem of goldenrod, then she bent over the canopy again. The beautiful man was still there, immobile, the back of his hand still brushing against the floor. He was strapped upright, his closed eyes calm, his face a thousand cracks held together by the strap under his chin.

Martha's hands searched the edges of the canopy again. She found no seam or opening. The craftsmanship exceeded anything she had ever seen—no rusted latches or gapped seams, no sign of rivet or bolt under the curve of her hands. He was dressed neatly and well shaved. Refined, a good man, a look of determination on his lips. The knife in Martha's hand dragged the surface and etched a spray of gashes, as if to leave an epitaph, maybe a flower, and suddenly Martha heard movement on the county road—something climbing, a distant sound of gears grinding, overdrive, rubber tires slipping on loose rocks.

"No," she cried out suddenly. "Not my glider."

Frantically, she picked up large clods of broken soil with grass growing out of the top and sides and threw them on the wings and fuselage. She tossed clumps at the glider. It wasn't enough. There wasn't enough time to camouflage the wings or the rudder sticking up like a gate without a fence. If Harold was coming, he'd rush in and rip open the canopy, chop it with an axe. He'd pull the gentle man out of the glider, pull him and flop him over his shoulder, reduce the man to a limp bag of potatoes slung over his shoulder. She ran to the canopy again and jabbed her fingers into the mud beneath the nose cone. A hook. She needed rope. Her tractor.

The seat of the tractor chilled her backside when she sat on the rusted metal. The tractor coughed and sputtered. "Come on, sonny," she shouted. The once blue vents on the sides of the tractor had paled to grey with rust. Martha jammed the throttle in and out, pumped the gas pedal, and stomped the clutch, trying to rouse some life into the machine that had been sitting under the lean-to for seven months. The cold surged into her tailbone, the winter still preserved in the metal. She pumped the gas pedal again and prayed to the pistons and the carburetor.

"Come on, sonny," she shouted to the albino blue tractor. "You can do it." The sound, the music of the engine. The tractor and Martha bumped over the bottomlands, through mud, up the incline, over the black soil. She backed it up to the glider's nose, grabbed the rope, and uncoiled it, the loops falling into loose circles. She tried to thread it through the tow hook buried in the mud. Unable to see. Her face flat against the glider's body while her arms groped through the mud for the hook. The eye of the hook. Poke. Pull. Run. Hurry. Back to the tractor, which idled while Martha tied knots. Back in the seat, on the cold metal again. It chilled her bowels while the sun pressed hot on her head, especially on the bare skin where she parted her hair.

The breeze from the rolling tractor dried the sweat from her cheeks as she towed the apparition of mud-covered white, tilting from side to side. The small wheels on the underside of the wing tips, which ordinarily kept the wings from dragging, jammed with grass and straw. Useless. The wings scraped the field, gathering pounds of debris, unwanted specimens of Martha's field.

In the warp of bright sun, Martha saw something moving in the distance, someone's truck slowing to turn off the county road, the right-turn signal blinking. But nothing was allowed on her property right now. She willed it away from herself.

She pulled faster, but the wing dragged, gathering more debris. The accumulated burden snapped the wing—five feet of it—into the field. The weight shifted to the shortened wing, dragging again, slowing the tractor as it labored toward the crest of Martha's field. If only she could get over the top.

The glider seemed to dig into the field, to bury itself. Martha jumped down from the metal seat and gaped at the swath she had cut. She ran along the towline toward the canopy and the man. She knocked on the plastic, rapidly, insistently. She pounded with the flats of her hands. "Open the canopy," she yelled. "Hurry. Let me in. Please."

The man was still, belted upright, unmoved by his journey across the field. His hand still brushed against the floor; his knuckles barely touched the mat. She pulled out her knife to gash all the way through the plastic, but it wouldn't yield, she couldn't cut to the heart of the thing. She pressed her cheek against the marred canopy and listened to herself gasp for breath.

Martha heard no sound except the click of the latch that she found. She pulled the man from the glider, his arms hanging from his sides, her elbows under his armpits. He unfolded onto the ground. She stumbled, pulling the man across the new and old green, inches at a time. He was heavy, past caring where he was taken. She pulled him through puddles, through standing water. His clean khaki pants were soaked with dark streaks of mud, his black boots mostly brown with twigs and dead grass fringing the soles.

On her front porch, she untied the laces on his boots. She loosened the X's, pulling them apart wriggling his boots from his feet.

Each button of his shirt, very carefully undone. Each round slipping through the buttonhole, no sound. His undershirt was dry, clean white. She unbuckled the belt, unsnapped the brass snap, and pulled carefully on the zipper's tab. An inch at a time, she loosened the pants from his hips, careful not to wake him, then from his thighs, pulling the fabric down, quietly, gently. His strong legs were matted with whorls of hair, flattened, mashed. His knees stuck out like mushroom caps. Hair on his shins. Hair at the tops of his ankles.

Martha held the muddied pants high in the air until they were aligned in proper creases, and she folded them, once, then twice. She buttoned the shirt, crossed the arms over the placket, and folded it in half, then in quarters.

The man was dressed in his flight helmet and clean underwear when Martha dragged him to the sofa, the softest place to rest. She pillowed his head and tucked him under an old quilt made from work clothes and plaid shirts.

She took a record out of its cardboard jacket and placed it on the turntable. A sweet solo violin played the opening notes of "The Lark Ascending" while Martha pulled the rocker to the sofa. She sat. She rocked. Sometimes, she reached over to touch his face, as if her fingers could warm the skin and erase the cracks, as if the puzzle of his face could be made whole.

Harold knocked at the door, his hat in one hand, his profile distorted through the beveled edge of the windowpane. He knocked, stood quietly, then knocked again. "Martha?"

She traced the outline of the leather helmet around the man's face. The clock, the pinched squeak of the rocking chair, the violin climbing to dizzying heights, and Martha's measured breath were the only sounds she heard.

White on White

After Don said he'd be home at six, Sara went out for a walk. She stopped to sniff a white rosebud and sit on a park bench. A man in a low-slung hat paced behind her, back and forth, his hands indecisive.

"I am a lady," she whispered to him, her elbow resting on the green slats of the bench. "I walk with my head high, toes and eyes pointed straight ahead, knees brushing together like models' knees to avoid the bow-legged look. I can keep five books on top of my head and still glide like a swan on smooth water."

The man stopped pacing.

"I am elegant, unruffled. I move to celestial music unbound by rhythmical form. In white," she continued, "I will greet my Maker."

The man in the hat ground his cigarette into the grass with his shoe, pulled up his collar, and put his hands in his pockets as he walked away.

Don gave Sara a red silk scarf with blue and orange stripes. "For you."

"I can't."

"Why not?"

Being a lady wasn't easy.

Her mother came to visit in her white car. She looked at the wilted Sara, sighed, and proceeded to dust the only Chinese Chippendale chair with a lace handkerchief.

"Remember who you are," she said, peering squarely into Sara's blue eyes. "Remember that you are a lady. You deserve the best. Demand it and don't give up on white."

She pressed a hundred-dollar bill into Sara's hand as she said good-bye. "For Mrs. Stewart's Liquid Bluing and something to wear."

* * *

On the day of the white sale, the snow falls upward, away from the earth, sucked by a white mouth, wider than the sky. Multilabial whiteness frames the horizons.

The lady's gloved hand brushes slowly over cutwork cloths, white web doilies, a wok with pearl inlay, and deckle-edged note paper. The white fingers stroke a bone-handled knife, the stainless blade. Overhead light shines on the alloy, reflecting white in the lady's eye at the white sale.

She stops at a window where pulsing light bulbs frame a wide-screen television covered with white-on-white dots. Ghost football. No bad news. A white horse leaps over the flashing crossbar and gallops to the north end of the shopping mall.

Sara's new suit is not stark white, but an off-white, more like ivory. The jacket has two cloth buttons, a softly tailored waist, and wide lapels. The skirt is slit and opens up to, oh, about middle thigh, seminoticeable when walking, very noticeable when sitting.

Sara's friend Madeline said, "Buy it."

"But the skirt has a slit, Madeline. Daring, wouldn't you say?"

"It's for you."

"But what will Don think? He's tired of white."

"You won't be sorry."

Sara checked in the three-way mirror three times. The off-white creamed her skin. But the margins of the mirror, the beveled edges that bent and distorted the reflection, framed some hesitation. She closed her eyes.

"A lady is as a lady does."

On weekdays Sara had worn white pinafores over white blouses to school. On Sundays, she had wiggled her stocking feet in the toes of white patent leather and laced her white-blond hair with white velvet ribbon. In the evenings she sat before starched white linen place mats and ate the white meat of turkeys and chickens and drank white milk. As she grew into a young woman, she rubbed lemon halves on her knees, elbows, and cheeks to coax the whiteness in her skin, but, despite all, she could not bleach herself as stark as her linens, voiles, and dotted-swiss cottons. She quietly observed the varieties and gradations of ladies from behind the whites of her eyes, imagining where she fit on the spectrum, and she still bought white, white as high noon on the desert, as grass underneath an abandoned board, as a spider's thread reflecting sunlight.

She opened her eyes. "I should, Madeline. You're right."

"Things are coming along," Don said, "slowly."

"Anything promising?" she asked.

"You can't pave the road to heaven with good intentions."

"I try, Don."

"Try harder. Everybody's got to try harder."

Sara waited to show him the suit.

White netting over a light-straw, broad-brimmed hat. White gloves. A long-sleeved, buttoned-to-the-elbow vision in cotton. Bodice laced tightly. Breasts gently rising, gently falling as the lady defined her breath ever so slightly. White gauze framing a white face—not pink, not beige. And the lady was gossamer, translucent, not really inhabiting the white floor-length gown that barely whispered over the polished wood. The gentleman called in his white, and they dined before the sun set. They walked on a sponge of air, sank softly into cushions as they exchanged white glances and sipped tea. She played with a pearl button at her neck, fingered the lace, rubbed it between two fingers, and he touched the rim of his white hat in the last light of the summer evening as the white changed to grey and he said good-bye, au revoir.

At first Sara wore a half slip under the skirt, and when she walked, the only thing anybody could see was the slit filled with white nylon and lace trim.

"Perfect," Don said as he tied the scarf around her neck with an overhand knot. She tossed her hair to act casual.

As time went by and when Don wasn't with her, she'd leave the red scarf and her half slip in the lingerie drawer. The satin lining in her well-tailored suit felt like a slip, anyway. She didn't need another one.

It was as if her left leg had a will of its own, like a disobedient child. She was often surprised by the way it sneaked out and tried to live a life of its own while she was standing there, surprised at her legs that could walk and run and take their owner to new places. It may have been the off-white or the slit, but when Sara wore her white suit and new white spaghetti-strap heels, her legs seemed to take over—Marilyn Monroe and *The Seven Year Itch,* World War II posters, long-legged pin-ups leaning back in rope swings twined with red and yellow flowers or resting their heads and shoulders against walls in dark smoke-filled rooms. It was as if they inched into operation, as if her appendages didn't cooperate with the trunk, the solid part of Sara, even in white.

"You won't mind if I don't wear the red scarf tonight, will you?" Sara asked.

"No," Don said, feeling full of oats and compromise. "Wear all the white you want. I'll even get you a white horse to ride."

They sat by a stained-glass window, and when Don stuck his straw in the waitress's cleavage after three gin and tonics, Sara excused herself to the ladies' room. She put her half slip in her purse, sat on a stool, crossed her legs, and pretended that she was Grace Kelly, the ultimate lady, and that some producer would see her legs and want to produce.

On the way back to the dining room, on the circular staircase, Sara stopped and struck a pose, one leg bent at the knee. Her leg flipped into an overhead kick and hung in the air suspended, toe pointed at the crystals on the chandelier.

"Madame, is there anything I can get for you?" the maitre d' asked.

"No, thank you," she said.

The leg started to circle, brushing the ground, arcing back to tickle the faceted crystal. Her leg: a propeller whose circumference swept the width of the staircase. No one could pass, but no one wanted to. They'd never seen a leg like that one.

"Who can can-can?" she asked the gathering crowd. "I can."

Bent knee, high kick, bent knee, high kick. Circle kick, turn, bounce. Ruffles up, derriere, ruffles down, back kick. Ta-ra-ra kick. Boom-de-a kick. The lady in the white suit covered the circular stairs, circling and whirling. All with one leg while the other stood staid, still, and serene.

Sara's mother bought her a white piano, had all the black keys removed and the empty spaces filled with natural sponge.

"For you, Sara. C-major forever. Tonic, tonic, diatonic. No accidentals, sharps, or flats."

Sara has never seen such a prize. Her canescent cat walks across the keyboard, stares into the white cracks, and its eyes contract. Pin-tip eyes. Lilied pointillism.

It's funny, in the white suit you'd think that Sara would be ladylike, all that cool pressed presence, the near whiteness.

She wore white at her wedding, of course. Sara's mother hovered until Sara remembered to carry the white crepe train over her arm while she nibbled white cake with white frosting and white roses out of Don's hand.

"Marry me," he had said. "Pledge to me, forever."

"Oh, forever, yes, of course."

"A bride is always beautiful," everyone said, "and Sara is the perfect bride, the perfect lady."

In white, Don and Sara held hands and smiled, even blushed. In white sheets they sanctified their holy calling of marriage. In white hospital gowns they held new babies and beamed. Sara wore white when she learned the correct backhand technique from the Yugoslavian tennis ace, when she learned to ski powder, and when she saw Don with his hand on the snow bunny's angoraed breast.

And she rode in white upon a white horse, charging through the dappled sunlight down the country lane. The light from the sun blanched the Persian rug by the window where she sat and rocked after the riding was done. It faded the flowered wool, fed on its color. And the table . . . the table has one dark circle where the geranium and its clay pot sat for sunning. The flower grew and died. The surrounding table bleached white. The whiteness is tight; it rings when it is tapped, the sound of crystal. And when the sun sets, the lady sees a star, pure flame burning itself to death.

White. A bride with cloth shoes and a spray of baby's breath braided into a crown. Sanitized bathroom sinks and toilets with an unbroken strip of paper winding around the seat. Space infused with light in an empty room free of impurities. Multitudes dressed in afterlife white to greet the newcomer who parts the veil, the redeemed in white neckties, awash in a sea of foam. White buttons on the baby's christening gown. A fish's belly, hospital sheets. Livid white. Lips tight with anger, knuckles clenched. White hair drained of pigment and imagination. The cheeks of a dead person.

And the lady rides again, the lady in white on a white horse. A white rabbit hesitates at the edge of the road. The lady reins the horse and three albinos greet one another—a rabbit and horse with pink eyes, a lady with rose-tinted lenses to protect her eyes from the white sun and the stars.

"Classy," that's what Anthony said when he saw her in the white suit for the first time. "A classy lady."

He knew.

"He's my cousin," she said, because she felt crazy and because people believed her in white.

Anthony knew how to treat a lady—with deference, holding doors and walking on the outside to protect the lady from mud that might splash. Anthony would have spread his cape for her to walk on if he had had one. And Anthony unbuttoned the cloth-covered buttons of her white suit with respect and hung the jacket carefully in his wardrobe.

"I am a lady," she said, wrapped in a white sheet.

"I know," he said.

Oh, Say, Can You See?

Over a radio microphone, into the nation's and Franklin Delano Roosevelt's ears, Grandma sang "The Star Spangled Banner." "Oh, say, can you see," she sang, my grandma who ironed for nickels and scrubbed for dimes, "by the dawn's early light, what so proudly we hailed. . . ." Everybody in Boulder City recommended her for the program because they'd heard her sing at funerals.

A big black open car full of VIPs delivered her home from the dedication ceremony. She waved good-bye to them, and they waved back. That's what my daddy told me.

I think she sang by the memorial, in between the statues—broad-chested men flanked by tall stiff wings pointing skyward. I hope those ninety-six men who died building the dam got fluffier wings or else they never will fly out of their graves.

More than anything, I remember the dam and that story about Grandma. But there was an atom bomb test, too—a rip in the sky by the dawn's early light, a gash that showed the sky's insides just for a minute. I thought about my metal Band-Aid box. I never could have unwrapped enough Band-Aids even if I pulled the red string exactly down the side crease without tearing into the flat side of the paper where the red letters are printed. After that minute passed, the sky's blood and the earth's dust made a big cloud, a busy one. It drifts over my mind sometimes.

I got my first chance at swearing because of Hoover Dam—"I went to the dam to get some dam water. I asked the dam man for some of his dam water and the dam man said no."

Damns were frowned on at my house. So I chanted the forbidden whenever I could, with a flourish, making sure Mama and Daddy heard.

Actually, we called it Boulder Dam. At one time or another, everybody talked about jumping off or sliding down the curving concrete, but nobody did it except one time a man from New York. His note said that he lost his money gambling in Las Vegas and that nothing mattered anyway.

"He looked like a mass of jelly," said Uncle Jack, an electrician at the dam.

"Could you see his face at all?" I asked.

"It was leaky, liquid in the cracks."

I wanted to ask more but my aunt changed the subject.

Whenever anybody came to visit we always took them to see the dam. Down to Black Canyon, down to 120 degrees in the shade where heat ricocheted off sizzling boulders.

Every time, even now, I stop at the memorial on the Nevada side. The two bronzed angels stand guard over a message: "It is fitting that the flag of our country should fly in honor of those men . . . inspired by a vision of lonely lands made fruitful. . . ." My sister used to say that some of them fell off scaffolds into wet, pouring cement. Concrete soup. I always looked to see if a hand or a foot stuck out anywhere in the dam and checked for bumps on the surface.

The cloud had bumps, swollen and bulging. I've seen many shapes of clouds in my life—lambs, potatoes, even alligators—but I saw only one like that lumpy mushroom. Its cap reminded me of the North Wind, the puffy-cheeked one who bets with the sun and blows fiercely to get coats off people's backs. Instead of sky and trees, it blew into the earth and got everything back in its face—sand, splintered tumbleweeds, thousands of years of rocks battering their own kind, crashing, colliding against each other, the dry desert silt, jaggedly rising from ribboned gullies and rain patterns on the sand, rising into a cloud that looked like a mushroom capped by the swollen-cheeked North Wind.

My father is proud of Hoover Dam. He helped build it, drove trucks hauling fill. He also loves the desert. Mama never thought much of it, probably never will.

"Horace, it's so hot here, so dusty. No creeks, no greenery. It's not human to live here."

My daddy always smiles when she starts in.

"Horace, can't we move before it's too late?"

Daddy never argues this subject. He just reminds Mama of his mother, the grandma who sang, and how she saved her family with a letter to her relative: "Can't find work. We've tried everything in the Great Basin—farming in Idaho, mining in Nevada, selling shoes in Utah. Thought you might have a place for my husband and sons helping on that big new dam."

"It seemed like we were heading for Mecca, it did," he used to say. "All those mirages on the highway and our tires never getting wet. Sunshine, wide open-armed skies, and promises."

"Promises? Of what?" Mama asked. "How can you cultivate rocks in Black Canyon, Hoover Dam cement, the sand, the sage, the yucca?"

"I have a job, a wife, three children, and an address," he said. "God bless the government."

The one time that Mama did leave the desert and the dam, the time when my father put on his Navy uniform with the brass buttons to go sailing in the Pacific, she didn't get treated like she should. Daddy always reminded her. Mother thought her relatives would help out with me and my sister Alice when she moved to Rupert, Idaho, but all extra hands were needed for milking, haying, harvesting potatoes.

"I'm sorry, but . . ." they all said.

Mama taught school—six grades in one room. She was tired at night when she picked me up from the scratch-and-bite nursery school for war orphans. She didn't talk much then, so I looked for Daddy under the covers, under the bed, and in the bathtub.

"Why did Daddy go away? Is he coming back?"

Mama read letters to us, words like China, Okinawa, kamikaze, Battleship Missouri, destroyers, phrases like "I miss you," "When the war is over," and "When we get back home to Boulder City, I'll roll down Administration Hill with Irene and Alice."

Rolling. Me rolling, repeating my face to the green grass. The cloud rolling, repeating itself to the open sky. And deep inside the busy cloud topped by the North Wind puffing in the wrong direction, a fire burned. Not a bonfire, but a tall fire hedged by a column of jumbled whites, browns, and greys, a thick fire mostly hidden but not quite. Black smoke twisted away from the red fire, sometimes losing itself in the confusion, sometimes slithering out into the blue. The cloud burned, scarring its belly, melting its insides with red and yellow while it rolled over and over in the same place.

We still pass Administration Hill every time we drive to the dam to go on the world's longest elevator ride, dropping down deep into the stomach, the belly of Hoover, to the hum of big red generators with white round lights on top.

The guide always talks about kilowatts, power to southern California, and spillover precautions. I used to watch the ant tractors and drivers circling the generators stories below while he explained.

"Now, if you will follow me, we will go directly into the Nevada diversion tunnel," a voice from a bullhorn said. Our feet echoed through a dripping cave, man-blasted, the voice said.

Water roared through a giant grey penstock (the guide called it) under the square observation room. I barely heard his speech. He pointed to yellow, red, blue, and green lines on a painted chart under a green metal lampshade. Outside the glassed, chicken-wired window, a man balanced on a catwalk to check bolts twice his size. The room trembled. The water rushed. I was glad that I didn't have to tightrope catwalks and check pipes as big as the world.

"If you will step this way, I will lead you to the base of the dam. Watch your step, ladies and gentlemen."

Outside, we looked up, up, up, everywhere up. Big cables stretched across, miles overhead—cables that lowered tons of railroad cars onto the tracks where we stood. I moved my toe quickly at the thought. Over the edge of the wall, the Colorado whirled green pools into white foam.

One time I told my mother that the river must be mad.

"Rivers don't get angry, Irene," she said.

"This one does. It doesn't like going through all those tunnels and generators. It would suck me down forever if I fell in."

"You won't fall in. Mother's here to protect you."

Reassured, I ran from the wall to the center point where I could spread-eagle across two states.

"Ma'am," blared the bullhorn, "will you kindly keep your child with the tour group?"

My mother jerked me back into Arizona, told me to stop wandering off, to stay with the group.

Once when I was about six, Uncle Jack scooped me into his arms. The temperature must have been 128 degrees that day.

"See, Irene, honey. See the steepest, longest slide on earth." He not only held me up, but held me over the edge to see better.

"Uncle Jack. Put me down." I kicked and squirmed.

"Not yet, honey. Look at the big river down there. We harnessed that river. We did it. Look. That's where you were a few minutes ago on the tour. See the railroad tracks?" He held me with only one arm as he pointed.

"Uncle Jack. Put me down, Uncle Jack. I don't like to look there." My head burrowed into his grey uniform but got stopped at the metal numbers on his badge.

"Come on, honey. Uncle Jack wouldn't let anything happen to you." He still held me out over the edge.

"Let me down. Let me down."

"Why are you so upset? I wouldn't . . ."

I ran away from his words, away to the car that boiled the closest two feet of air around its metal surface. The door handle was untouchable, unopenable. I couldn't hide away to cry. I had to do it in the air, on top of that dam, in front of people from Manila, Cheyenne, and Pittsburgh.

I used to wonder if there had been devils in that red-fire cloud. My mother always talked about devils liking fire and red and gambling, even how the world would end by fire because of them. I imagined horns balancing on top of their red caps that buttoned tight, holding all that cunning close between their ears while they rolled and tumbled in the churning clouds, while the fire burned yellow and red at the center and in my eyes when I thought about it.

One night after Uncle Jack held me out over the dam, he and my mother balanced a bed on the overhead cables, thousands of feet above concrete and water.

"You have disobeyed again," Mama said. "Always running off."

"I'm sorry."

"You'll have to sleep out there tonight, Irene. Maybe you'll learn to listen."

"Please, Mother, not at the dam. I'll be good. I'll listen. I won't go away without telling you ever again."

''Just climb up the ladder, honey,'' said Uncle Jack. ''Nothing to worry about.''

''Please, no,'' I said as I climbed the ladder, up, up, high above the scenic viewpoint where tourists stood with gaping mouths. The wind blew, the cables rose and fell and twirled jump rope. I wore my blue furry Donald Duck slippers and my rosy chenille bathrobe, and I put one and then another foot ahead, in front. For a minute I walked on the wind and wasn't afraid. Then I got to that creaking bed, leaning downside at every shift in weight.

''Rock-a-bye, baby,'' Mama sang. ''Hush-a-bye.'' Uncle Jack accompanied her on his trumpet.

The bed started to slip. The bedsprings scraped over the cables, fingernails on a blackboard, slipping one by one.

''Mama,'' I screamed.

Mama leaned as far out over the edge as she could while Uncle Jack held her knees. We stretched for each other. Like long, rubbery, airless balloons, we stretched and stretched, arching, reaching, trying to connect.

''Hold me, Mama.''

Our fingertips only pointed at each other as I passed.

I tried to make a sail out of the quilt. I stood up to catch the wind with it but couldn't keep my balance. One Donald Duck slipper, followed by the other, followed by me in rosy chenille, sailed through the night toward the dam to get some dam water from the dam man.

After it mushroomed, the cloud started to break apart and dot the sky. I remembered the time I climbed a leafless tree. Instead of watching where I was climbing, I talked to Rocky, my dog, who jumped and yelped at the bottom. Someone else had broken the twig that raked my cheek, that beaded the slash with red. A necklace of red pearls, almost. Dot dash dot. A design that stared at me in the mirror until it got better and faded away just like the cloud did.

Everybody wants to see the dam. It's famous. One day when I was about ten, another big black car, open and full of important men again, drove through Boulder City. Flags stuck out on both sides of the windshield, rippling. I tried every possible angle to see Ike, running around legs, pushing through to openings but finding none. I was missing everything. Everybody who had closed shop and home for the afternoon was crowding to see Ike, too.

"Daddy, hold me up so I can see."

His dark blue uniformed arms full of baby brother, he pointed to the sill of Central Market's picture window. Stacks of returnable glass bottles towered behind the pane and wiggled every time a reflected parade watcher moved.

I climbed to the ledge as the fire engine and two police cars passed, sirens blaring. Even standing there, I could see only flashing red lights, the backs of heads, and an occasional helium balloon drifting, ownerless.

"Daddy, I can't see."

Somehow, he managed to pick me up in time. Ike, his uniform dotted with brass and ribbons, looked just like the Newsreel pictures at the Boulder Theatre. He smiled and waved just like on Newsreel, too. I didn't need to see him after all. I already knew.

I liked the high-school band best. The flags and the band.

"Children," my father said at the dinner table that night, "you are lucky to live in America." His blue eyes became moist as they always did when he talked about God and country. We all knelt by our chairs and Daddy said, "We thank thee for such men as General Eisenhower to lead our great country. Bless our friends and relatives. Help us to live in peace. Amen."

I saw Ike again on Newsreel several weeks later. He was still waving and smiling, framed by the granite-like building blocks of the dam. He didn't look too big next to the dam. Neither did his friends.

One morning, about five o'clock, our grey Dodge drove in the opposite direction from the dam, toward Las Vegas, out by Railroad Pass where Uncle Jack played trumpet on Saturday night. Alice and I kept warm under a Log Cabin quilt and traced the zig-zagging pattern changes with our fingers, waiting.

"It's time," Daddy said. "Watch. Don't miss this. We should be able to see everything, even if it is seventy-five miles away."

We waited some more, eating apples and crackers.

"It's got to be time," he said.

My neck crabbed. I looked at the sunrise.

"There it is, there it is," he yelled.

I saw the flash, but mostly my father's face and his brass buttons that seemed to glow red for one instant.

"That's how I came home to you, everybody. Just look at that power."

The cloud flowered, mushroomed, turned itself inside out, and poured into the sky. Red fire burned in the middle of browns and greys, colors that hid the red, almost. But it was there—the fire burning at the center, the red fire that charred the North Wind's puffed cheeks and squeezed eyes until it blew itself away, trailing black smoke and its pride. It was there in the middle of the rising columns of earth and clouds boiling over, clouds bursting into clouds, whipping themselves inside out, changing colors over and over. Red, yellow, and black, colors from the fire. Grey, brown, and beige, sand from the desert floor, Daddy said.

And then the picture blurred at its edges, unfocused itself into other shapes—smoke arches, long floating strings, dots and dashes. In no time at all, everything floated away, on the jet stream, Daddy told us.

"I thought it would last longer," I said, "Won't they do it again?"

Daddy laughed. "It's time to go home now and get some hot breakfast. Wasn't that amazing, kids?"

Everyone who had gotten up to watch the blast talked about it in school that day. "Did you see it?" Our desert land had been chosen once again for an important government project.

The front page of that night's newspaper ran pictures of the before and after—frame houses before, no frame houses after; dummied soldiers before, no recognizable dummies after. Surprised cattle lay flat out in the dead grass on their sides, their hair singed white on the up side. Yucca Flats. Frenchman Flats. Mercury Test Site. Household words.

"Nobody can get us now," my daddy said.

I don't think about it much, but sometimes when I rearrange my pillow for more fluff, ready to settle into sleep, the cloud mists into long, red, airy fingers over everything, reaching across the stark blue.

Trees

I heard my trees screaming last night. They were chopped into branches. Slain, dead, broken, sawn, bleeding on the street in front of my house—especially the white birch.

The trees had been healthy. They were enjoying a long life when I invited the man with the chain saw to my house. "This one, that, and that one," I said, pointing my finger to each unsuspecting giant in my yard.

"It's too dark in my house," I explained to the man with the wine-colored T-shirt and sweat band.

"We need some sunlight," I told his assistant. "Their branches are hiding us from everybody, inviting burglars."

The men grunted and pulled cords that brought their saws to life—the saws that they carried in orange, violin-looking cases. I thought they were members of some musical ensemble when they first arrived, coming to play music for me.

The trees towered over us until one of the saws gashed the middle of one so deeply that it fell to its knees, one knee left, one knee filled with history, rings, sap, juice, one naked knee of a tree. Someone counted twenty-eight rings, but the trees were older than that. I felt their age in my bones.

The saws buzzed so loudly that there was no quiet place in my house. The noise carved up my ears, cut into more trees, insisted and insisted as the vibrating chain hacked into the centers and cores and lives of my trees.

The birch tree screamed the loudest—in fact, I can still hear the echoing in my house. Tree screams are more insistent than mortal screams, at least they last longer. Higher, more piercing, penetrating, they roll out into oxygen and back again.

I loved my trees. I meant to hug them good-bye. I did kiss the ash and the bristly branch of the pines, but then I forgot to go to the front yard for the white birch. It's not going to forgive me. I can feel it. How can I get it to forgive me now? It's in so many pieces.

Love Story for Miriam

I've finished my visit with Hortense, the great-aunt who's always been my favorite and who doesn't have much life left in her pocket. Standing just inside the multipurpose room of the God Bless You Rest Home, I watch her sister Miriam, who's a crack in the family armor, a slight mystery, a slight joke.

She plays "Red Sails in the Sunset" on an upright piano long separated from standard pitch and is oblivious to the old duffers in wheelchairs who are diapered, bibbed, tied to the IV lines and catheter bags. She doesn't seem to hear anything, not even the loud barks of the nurses' aides in the hall.

"Oh, carry my loved one," she sings with a vibrato someone could walk through, "home safely to me."

"Miriam," the nurse inserts between musical phrases, "It's time for your juice."

She smiles at the nurse with her mouth only, a twitch of a smile with quick corners. Her eyes seem lost in harbor mist.

"He loved me."

"Your juice, Miriam."

"Edward Titley loved me," she says to the nurse, "but I didn't like the name Miriam Titley."

"Miriam, you need your juice," the nurse insists, "and you can't drink it by the piano. It might spill between the keys. Over here."

She pats the ancient Naugahyde chair, its back covered by a black afghan with multiflowered squares.

"Come on, Miriam," the nurse says, never once losing her professional patience.

"Where's Hortense?"

"Come on, honey." The nurse pats the chair with two hands.

The piano bench complains when Miriam pushes it out from under herself. It chugs across the linoleum checkerboard and leaves a fresh black scar in its wake. Immaculately dressed in color coordinates and chewing her dentures ever so slightly, Miriam carries herself at a tipped angle across the just-dried wax. She practices air piano as she walks, and her paste jewels play light tag with the neon tubes overhead.

"Enjoy yourself," says the nurse as soon as Miriam settles into the chair.

"Where's Hortense? I want my sister." Her voice quavers like a late-night, long-distance radio station.

"In her room, resting."

"Why doesn't she come in and sing with me? 'Red Sails' is one of her favorite tunes."

"She doesn't feel well, dear."

I watch the woman who's supposed to be my flesh. She's sipping orange juice in an afghan-covered chair and is dressed for high tea. In my memory I can feel her closeness to my once young cheek, her prudish kiss a bare whisper on my flesh, my sensing of her absence even then. Miriam. A lost child meandering through the forest of her mind, Miriam who wanders away before she arrives, who looks for her place and forgets she's looking, who feels safe only when she is next to Hortense.

When I asked Grandma Jean about Miriam, wanting to know what made her the way she is, she said their mother took great pride in Miriam when she was a little girl. Cherished her crystal-goblet delicacy. Brushed Miriam's hair every night like it was God's talent to be multiplied. "Pretty child, pretty angel," their mother always said to Miriam.

"When Mother pressed the spines of the hairbrush too hard into her scalp, Miriam would say, "Careful, Mama. I'm your angel, remember."

"I wouldn't hurt my angel," Mother would say as she covered her rough red fingers with kisses and patted them into Miriam's hair."

On Sundays, Grandma Jean told me, their mother braided and looped Miriam's hair into a crown, shined her black patent shoes with a soft towel, and buttoned them onto her feet. Then she slipped tiny pearls on the dearly bought lace dress into loops of twisted thread while Jean and Hortense tied each other's cotton sashes. Then, on the way to Sunday School, the older sisters would walk behind Miriam to form a triangle, their mother patting tiny Miriam on the shoulders like she was the sharpest point of the triangle, like she was Queen of the May.

Even at age nine, Grandma Jean said, Miriam held court on the overstuffed chair in the living room, flanked by two dolls in white lace caps.

''One day I remember especially,'' Grandma Jean said. ''Her bounteous red hair was wrapped in rags. That's how Mother made those plump sausage ringlets, you know. I think she had a piano recital that afternoon. She sat there like royalty while Hortense and I tracked a cockroach across the floor. 'You're not ladies,' Miriam told us. Hortense never did pay her much mind. 'Who says?' she snapped at Miriam, all the time keeping her nose buried in the rug and her derriere kingdom high while she followed that cockroach. 'Ladies don't chase bugs.' Miriam lifted her teacup with her little finger crooked and drank imaginary tea. 'I'm different from you and Jean,' she said. 'I wish you could see what I see.' 'I'm getting sick,' Hortense told her, sticking out her tongue. 'Of you.' 'Don't say that,' Miriam said, leaning her head on her arm that was draped over the back of the chair.''

''Miriam was a beauty, I'll say that much for her. The tendons in her neck stretched long and graceful like a swan's when she rested her head like that on the chair. I remember that picture of her like it happened yesterday. 'It's beautiful inside my mind,' she told Hortense. 'Like jewels and rubies in a glass palace.' 'Oh, really?' Hortense said like she sometimes does. A little uppity. 'Clusters of crystal jut out from the walls like lanterns, Hortense. Sparks of light that can blind a stranger if she's not careful. Everything glitters behind my eyes, and there's the most angelic music.' Hortense kept following the cockroach even though I decided I wasn't interested any longer. Then, she walked on her knees across the rug, imitating the insect feelers with both her arms. 'Look at me, Miriam.' She knelt next to the green chair, her arms waving through the air. 'Do I have flashes of light on me? Do I sparkle, too?' And Miriam stroked Hortense like she was our pet cat. 'Your hair is silk,' she said. 'Strands of silk. Lights in your hair, Hortense, moving up and down the strands.' 'You're weird, Miriam. When are you going to stop being weird?' Hortense ran for the hall door, motioning me to follow her to our favorite hideout where

Miriam wasn't welcome. 'Let's get out of here.' Poor Miriam just sat in the chair covered with those Egyptian plumes. She was as poised as a storybook doll except she kept saying 'No one can hurt me,' over and over until she closed her eyes to keep her world intact. 'I'm not like you.' "

"No doubt about it. Miriam's always been strange," Grandma Jean concluded. "Not demented, mind you. Just lives in her own peculiar world."

I didn't tell Grandma Jean that I've seen similar rooms in my head, rooms carved of ebony with strings of gemstones for light. I've sometimes dreamt of living on a planet carpeted with stars, or fancied myself a reincarnated princess out of Egypt. And I hear music when there isn't any outside of myself, just like Miriam does. If I'm honest, I'd say Miriam isn't so dumb—everyone taking care of her, picking up after her, handling all the unpleasantries. But I don't mention my feelings to anyone in the family. There's always Miriam to be compared with, and I don't especially want that to happen. She's something of a canceled check to most of the relatives.

My mother thought the explanation for Miriam might be the way her mother never could stand still. Her father was a mellow man who took time to savor life. But every night while he sat quietly in his easy chair sipping hot chocolate and reading poetry, his wife zipped from corner to corner, frantically scattering dust and reminding him he should be doing something besides sitting there in that chair. She ran to the neighbors with funeral casseroles or baby booties she'd crocheted, and she sang for everybody's special occasion. While she did all these good works, she pulled Miriam by the hand from one place to the next, always rushing to be necessary to someone. Maybe it was the wooden pews Miriam sat on while she waited for her mother to practice with the choir. Maybe their hardness summoned fantasy to rescue her. Maybe her legs hung over the edge and couldn't touch the floor. That might have given her a feeling of escape from gravity even then.

Maybe Miriam felt like a feather grabbed out of the air and tucked in her mother's pocket to show off to friends. "How pretty. How delicate." Vanes of the feather catching the breeze as her mother moved rapidly through town on her sturdy black shoes, always saying yes when someone asked a favor even if she didn't want to, always responding to the demands of the outer world, always moving too quickly for Miriam.

Miriam in slow motion. In stop time. Miriam entrenched, rooted to the air. An exercise in opposition.

Even though I have an appointment in ten minutes, needing to run to the next obligation just like Miriam's mother did, I can't leave this multipurpose room or stop watching Miriam. She looks like a royal dowager in the run-down armchair with two books propped underneath in place of a missing leg. I lean against the frame of the wide door and feel the swamp cooler blowing in my face.

"Don't be like Miriam" was the family maxim. "You don't want to end up like her. Helpless. Childless. A burden to Hortense." My sisters and I were duly warned. "Don't be so choosy. So self-centered. You'll end up with nothing."

After she finishes her orange juice, she walks back to the piano. She pulls the bench out again, slides in front of middle C, and starts to play "Red Sails" again. She sings this time. "He sailed at the dawning, All day I've been blue." A few patients in the multipurpose room join in when she comes to the refrain, clap their hands together like prayers, and attempt to keep time to the music. I see John Lattimer, a former district judge, rolling in her direction in his wheelchair, his mouth wide open as if anticipating fine romance. Miriam doesn't notice him. He could be a fly for that matter.

Sitting on a wooden piano bench, entertaining the inattentive audience, she's impervious to their complaints or conditions. She could be the piano player in a lounge, actually. Surrounded by the rising smoke and dim lights and performing for the fuzzy minds of late-night drinkers. She seems fathomless sitting there, placeless, out of time. And then I hear John Lattimer asking her if she knows how to play "Yankee Doodle Dandy."

His tight, marbled skin stretches across his knuckles and across the bridge of his nose where little red veins wriggle like ant trails. He wears a one-piece diaper/bib combination over his blue plaid shirt and grey wash slacks, and white hairs sprout from his ears and nose. He sings along. "A real live nephew of my Uncle Sam, born on the Fourth of July. . . ."

Cousin Ted was the one who moved the sisters out of their apartment into the nursing home. ''Hortense's heart and Miriam's worry,'' he told me at the family reunion in Memory Grove, a week after he'd finished the transfer.

''That Miriam's always fretting about things that never happen.'' Ted gripped a frosted can of Cherry 7-Up in one hand and a Kentucky Fried Chicken wing in the other.

'' 'Someone's after me,' she told me when Thelma and I visited with her just before the move. 'They're going to break into my room,' she said in that shaky voice she has. How does somebody's voice get like that, anyway?''

''I don't know,'' I said, holding a limp paper plate full of potato salad, sliced raw vegetables, and Ted's wife Thelma's special baked beans with pineapple tidbits and bacon.

''I assured her she was in a well-protected location, but right then Hortense started in.'' Ted laughed as he ripped the crispy skin from the wing with his teeth. ''She's such an old salt even though she's got the biggest heart in the universe. She started in on how Miriam is just dying to have somebody break in and seduce her. She made some great crack about Miriam waiting around for a hundred years, just like Sleeping Beauty. It was all I could do to keep my face straight.''

Ted patted his pleasant belly, rotated the 7-Up can in his hand, and laughed hard for the time he couldn't when he was with the sisters.

'' 'But men do break in and hurt women sometimes,' Miriam said to me, sitting up tall on the sofa to wield a little authority. 'I read the newspapers.' And then that sharp old tack, Hortense, tells her she's been starved for a beau ever since she decided she was too good for Edward Titley. Those two just crack me up, I tell you.''

I crunched into my carrot stick. ''I don't know how they've managed all these years,'' I said to Ted.

''Miriam just didn't have the strength to face the world.'' Ted picked up the barrel of chicken and offered me a breast. ''Last piece. Want it?''

''You still look hungry, Ted. It's yours.''

''If you say so.''

"Sometimes," I said, "I think they both needed each other. Hortense needed Miriam to be weak to prove she was strong."

"That's hogwash," Ted told me. Then he rolled out a round sort of laugh from deep inside. "Nobody needs Miriam! You know how I've got my new condo. Sauna. Hot tub. Well, I invited Miriam to come for a visit, but she kept insisting she couldn't leave her sister alone. 'You don't know how much Hortense needs me,' she said. She sat there, real pitiful-like, holding that Baby Tears doll Hortense gave her for Christmas."

"Thelma told her she'd been cooped up too long in that apartment and needed sunshine. Old Miriam wiggled her painted toes in those big pink ostrich-feather slippers she wears and asked if she could bring her baby. Before I made some dumb remark like I do sometimes, good old Thelma told her we have plenty of room for her baby since our kids are grown and gone. I'm glad there's at least one diplomat in the family."

Miriam. Is she just a mildewed clock that keeps different time or does she know something the rest of us don't? If I use some logic gleaned from my domestic experience, a baby doll stays the same smiling child forever. It doesn't grow up and talk back. Its voice doesn't change, it doesn't grow breasts and howl at the moon for someone to mate with. Why not dedicate a life to a doll who never soils a diaper or spits up on clean clothes? Why should the baby or Miriam spoil themselves?

I've asked everyone—Ted, Grandma Jean, Hortense, my mother—about Miriam and Edward Titley, but it seems like a closed topic for some reason, like they were shadow puppets on a shade. The standard story is that Miriam was too good for his name, even though he was a devout Christian and groomed himself in a gentlemanly way. I can picture her turning her hands in her lap from back to front while Edward leaned forward to ask.

"I can't explain, Edward, but I have to say no."

"But I thought we had an understanding," he might have said.

"I made no promises."

"But you kissed me," he might have insisted. A woman kisses a man, and he thinks he has some territorial claim on her. She kisses him with any kind of passion, and he thinks she is ready, hook, line, and sinker. What if Miriam just liked to kiss? What if she said, "I like kisses, but I can't love."

"Everybody can love," Edward would have said, his courage returning because he believed in Jesus, fishes and loaves and love most of all. "I'll help you learn about love. No human being can live without it."

And maybe Miriam asked Edward Titley, "Just what are human beings? I'm waiting to find my way back to something more real than this. Something more reliable. Why do I need you?"

Poor Edward! I can imagine him leaning against the cabinet radio, his watch chain connecting his two vest pockets, his pale moustache fading into a pale complexion. "But you accepted my flowers and chocolates . . . and my kisses."

"I like all of that," she would have said, "but why do you need to possess me? You'd only want me to be different than I am, Edward, so why take me at all?"

And Edward would be confounded, wanting to wrap her in a package he could carry under his arm, wanting her to be cooperative and predictable. I don't blame him actually, who doesn't want life to be predictable? But where's the room for Miriam, who lives by some abstract set of rules conceived by devotees of floating dreams, who's now looking over at me while she sings about dandies and the Fourth of July? Does she remember me? Remember I'm her niece, her blood relative? She looks like she sees right through me, sees all the things I can hide from other people. What does Miriam see as she seems not to be seeing me? Her look is not a burrowing stare. It goes through and beyond me, and I feel blown like glass, my insides visible.

Once I asked Hortense to tell me about her sister, though it wasn't easy because Miriam was always around when I visited and because Hortense usually wouldn't talk about her. But one day when Miriam had a headache and went to lie down, I sat by Hortense on the sofa to help fold her clean clothes. She put the overflowing basket on the floor in front of us, and for some reason, she talked about Miriam, something she rarely did.

"She moved in with us when Rube and I lived in San Francisco. She slept most of the time. For a while, she worked as a sales clerk in women's fashions at the City of Paris, but she couldn't keep the job. She'd tell all the ladies when a dress didn't look good on them. The manager thought that was bad policy. He apologized to each customer right in front of Miriam. He insulted her sense of style. Didn't understand her.''

Hortense told me that after Miriam lost her job she'd wander out to the beach and watch the sailboats. Maybe she contemplated the boats, but I suspect it was the water beneath them. She wondered if there might be someone waiting for her there, a kindred spirit, someone who saw the world like she did.

When she climbed back up the hill to her sister's apartment, she probably watched for turning door knobs on row houses or for the space between gauze curtains in bay windows where an extended finger might curl and invite her inside. She must have watched for hands or faces that would say, ''Miriam, here we are. We've been waiting for you. Come home.''

''Our stairs were steep,'' Hortense said to me while she folded a dish towel made from a flour sack. ''She'd be out of breath after she closed the front door. 'Miriam,' I'd call. 'I'm in the kitchen.' Miriam would hang her cardigan on the hall tree. Come in all neat and tidy while I had wet curls swimming down my neck. There she'd be with that string bag, her contribution of crab and sourdough, every Friday. 'Miriam, I can't go on like this,' I told her. 'I've got the babies and a sick husband. Bread and crab once a week isn't enough.' 'I make my bed, Hortense,' she'd always say. 'I wash my own clothes and stay out of the way.' I chopped carrots, trying to hide my anger, but that day it just came out of my mouth. I even yelled at her that time. 'What about doing something for me?' I screamed at her. 'Ask yourself what might make me happy for a change.' Then she looked at me with those grey-violet eyes, large like a baby bird's, her eyelashes mascaraed like cartoon sunrays. Then I said the one thing I wish I'd never said. 'I don't need another baby, Miriam.' That's what I said to her.''

As she stacked the last towel on the pile, Hortense's eyes looked so sad. Nets wishing to retrieve all the words cast out to sea, words lost to the ocean, careless words. ''I love her, you know.''

''I think I do, too,'' I told her before I noticed the clock and remembered the next place I had to run to. ''Can I put the linens in the ironing for you?''

''No, dear. You've got to get back to your children. They need you, you know.''

Why do they need me? They'd be better on their own, actually. I love them because of duty and guilt, except for when they're asleep. Safe. Wrapped in nocturnal arms, which are so big and roomy. What kind of gift am I giving if I don't know how to love?

Does Miriam understand duty? Certainly not guilt. I've never seen her run anywhere or heard her say she should be going. Somehow she's suspended above the rest of us, given to the spaces above gravity. How did she become a marionette who totally trusted the strings for her every move, no effort necessary on her part? I'm tempted to say something about the lilies of the field, how they toil not, neither do they spin, but why should others take care of Miriam? How much can she take from everybody before the strain's too great? How much is she supposed to give back in return for her life?

I've seen Hortense and Miriam together many times, but my visits have mainly been to see Hortense, the strong, self-willed great-aunt who seemed like an anchor for Miriam, me, and so many others. She's been a stalwart for Miriam, giving her a place to live all these years, protecting her from the sharks in the water. She's a rock for all her brothers and sisters and cousins—the emotionally wounded, the recovering alcoholics, the bereaved—and for me when I thought I should leave my husband, who expected endless generosity without an equal return.

But maybe, as I told Ted, Miriam was the essential ingredient that made Hortense capable of so many burdens, her frailty giving Hortense an amplified notion of her strength. Maybe Miriam's strength that looked like weakness shaped Hortense. Made her long-suffering and generous and selfless like most of us pretend to be.

Ah, Miriam.

Usually they kept the peace when I visited, but one day I was helping them bottle peaches. They must have forgotten me standing over the kettle and the steam when we all heard the plate hit the floor.

"You've finally done it," said Hortense, her sudsed hands dripping above the water, her last piece of wedding china lying in pieces on the floor. "You've outlived my husband and now my china. Thanks a lot. Thanks. Just thanks."

Miriam held up a broken triangle. "It slipped. I didn't mean it to happen."

"You never mean to do anything, Miriam." Hortense pulled the stopper out of the drain. "For harm or good. You live in a powder jar."

"You're mad at me." Miriam's lips trembled. A red-cheeked, aging princess.

"I'm beyond mad, Miriam. How can anyone get mad at their own body, their flesh?"

"I'm not you. You're not me. We're different."

"I know, I know. You've told me before." Hortense wiped the suds from the sides of the sink and sprinkled cleanser on the procelain.

"You act so smart," said Miriam. "You make Ted and Thelma laugh at me when they visit. You make Jean mad, telling her I think I'm better than everybody. That's not fair. Nobody's smart who makes people laugh or become angry at other people."

"Shut your flapping trap, Miriam. Would've been better if you'd never opened it."

"Hortense. You're rude!"

"It's a hard life."

"I'm going into my room until you calm down."

Out of the corner of my eye, I saw Miriam fold the dish towel over the back of the kitchen chair. Her charm bracelet tangled at her wrist. "I didn't mean to hurt your plate," she said as she pushed up her sweater sleeves. The gold charms rattled like a chorus of "ayes" for Miriam—a ballerina on point, a Dutch maiden with both hands on her waist, a kitten rolling over a ball of yarn, a quarter note, an open rose, a heart with a slot for a key, the key that opened the heart—charms Hortense had given to Miriam one by one on her birthdays, all starting with the gold chain bracelet.

"Don't come back and finish the dishes, please," Hortense said, swiping at beads of water with the dishrag.

Miriam slammed the door of her room. Then she opened it and slammed it again. "Mean," she yelled, though her hothouse lungs had little power. The word sounded insubstantial. "Rude. You've always been rude."

"I'm sorry you're seeing this, Madeline." Hortense remembered me for one instant before she dragged her feet into the living room and dropped into the overstuffed chair—the one with a raised motif of plumes like the slaves used to wave over Pharaoh's head, the same chair Miriam used to hold court in when she was nine years old.

"Childless. Helpless. Useless," she said in a voice not loud enough to carry into the bedroom. "She'd die if I left her alone. Damn thing would die. Just lie down in the middle of the floor and evaporate." Hortense sighed a long, fatigued sigh. And then her eyeglasses fogged, and I saw the moisture on her cheeks.

The bedroom door creaked open. The sound of soft house slippers brushed across the sculptured carpet in the hallway, one slow step at a time. The footsteps moved closer to Hortense in the armchair. I tried not to, but I saw Miriam peeking around the hall corner like an ostrich, her eyes ringed with dark black smudges, a new application of red rouge stark on her face.

"I didn't mean anything I said, Hortense. You didn't mean anything either, did you?"

Hortense shook her head, her hands covering her face, her fingers underneath her eyeglasses.

"I really was born on the Fourth of July," John Lattimer is telling Miriam. "My mother taught me that song when I wasn't any higher than a grasshopper's knee."

He reaches over and pats Miriam on her knee. She slides out of his reach.

"You must have been a real doll," he says, squeezing the edges of her kneecap. She lifts his hand back into his own lap.

"John, you're so cute," she says as she chews her upper dentures back into place and pinches his cheek, "but my body is a temple. It's a sacred, holy place."

The insistent smell of urine mixes with the undiluted Pine-Sol being scrubbed onto the hall floors. Miriam covers her mouth to quiet a burp and looks into John's eyes.

He touches her hand.

"Where'd you learn to play the piano like that, Mimsey?"

"That's not my name, John, and stop touching me so much."

"It fits you." He chucks her chin.

"My mother wanted me to be a concert pianist."

"A fine profession."

"I liked performing," she says, pushing up the sleeves of her cardigan. "I played in some piano recitals."

"Play something now, just for me. Play 'Yankee Doodle Dandy' again, you fine woman."

Miriam rolls a full-piano-length arpeggio. "I'm a Yankee Doodle Dandy," John sings heartily. "Yankee Doodle, do or die."

Several vague and indirect voices trail along, sounding like the wind rising and falling back. Some sing their own version of the song, their own words about their own troubles.

The nurse walks up behind John and places her hands like epaulets on his shoulders.

"You two having a nice time?" She rearranges the shawl that has fallen behind his back.

"Mimsey's quite a gal," says John. He rubs his knees.

"Your niece is waiting, Miriam," the nurse says. "Would you like to see her?"

Miriam lifts her fingers from the keyboard. "Where's Hortense?"

"You know she's not as strong as you are, Miriam. Play some more music, dear. Everybody is singing."

"They need me, don't they?"

"Of course, dear." The nurse lifts Miriam's hand into her own and looks over at me. I walk over to Miriam at the piano, and the nurse places my great-aunt's hand in mine.

"Hello," I say. "Remember me?"

She chews her dentures for a few seconds and studies my face. "You look like my nephew, Barney."

"He's my father."

"That's nice," she says, and pulls her hands from mine.

John Lattimer pats her knee one last time. " 'Bye, you doll," he says, rolling away in his wheelchair.

I slide in next to her. "Who are you, Miriam? Really . . . who are you?"

She looks at me directly for a brief second and then her eyes slide into a faraway place. "I'm visiting the planet."

A few years ago I might have laughed, at least inside, but now, I don't. "Miriam, tell me about yourself."

She stands and pushes back the piano bench. She looks at me but not at me and smiles with the corners of her mouth.

"Miriam, please won't you say something?"

"You'd just want to change me. It was nice of you to visit, dear. Tell Barney hello for me, will you?"

She pats my shoulder and walks away in a halting manner, not totally sure of her step. Like a sloop with faded red sails, she rocks slightly, yet stands tall and erect like the mast. I watch her drift away, no anchor holding her. She glides away in her peculiar vessel, and I know I want to love this woman somehow, yet don't know what to love. Where can I connect if there are no handholds or footholds? Motel Miriam. Always vacant.

Maybe she is an angel, a real one without body, parts, or passion, a reminder of the great beyond where no one feels anything. Maybe someone assigned her this lonely part, and she plays it to remind us. To remind me to love my chance to be human and not try to escape too soon.

Argument

These kitchen knives have split chicken breasts.

They have minced livers, halved lemons, and ripped skin from pears.

There is no food that tastes in this kitchen, so I'll try the knives. I'll grate slivers of steel for the nutmeg on your eggnog. I'll shave edges of Gillette Blue Blades and embed them in green peppers on your pizza.

No blades will twist into your heart, only shards, tiny fragments prickling at your esophagus, your stomach lining, your intestines.

* * *

This keeps you answering, this paper money that covers your breasts with lace and pearls, fills your gaping mouth with oysters and bread, satisfies your outstretched hand.

I'll stuff your cavity with these bills, then truss you. I'll crumble the wads tight and drop them down your gullet one by one, clothespins in the milk bottle. I'll tear them into flakes and collage your eyes, and you'll never stop seeing the color that drives you to dance and sing and say pretty words.

Green glued to your belly, crocheted to your pantyhose, braided in your hair as you lie in state.

Criminal Justice

I need to tell you this before I tell you about that. I've baked lots of bread, nursed babies, and made quilts. I send thank-you notes and vote (even worked in two senatorial compaigns) and will do almost anything to avoid anger. Once upon a time, those things meant you were a good person, and I try to be good. I try hard. What else do I need to tell you before I talk about Highway 89 and those Highway Patrol cars?

Maybe I should admit I don't believe in heroes. The blacks and whites of my childhood are grey now, spattered with exposés of presidents and major-league ballplayers. And everybody seems to be carrying a handgun. Funny, I'm pausing, wondering why I try so hard to be good if I don't believe in it anymore . . .

Anyway, I've been as honest as I know how to be. People believe me because I'm tall and have an uptown face. One time when I suggested I'd like to be a migrant worker for a summer just to see what it was like—buy a rusted out Oldsmobile and follow the crops—my friends laughed and said no one would believe me. "It's the way you carry yourself. It's your aristocratic nose."

Whatever it is, I'm used to being dealt with respectfully, so when Patrolman Littlefield tells me to bend over and put my hands on the trunk of the car, I am confused. I'm bending over the trunk of a car I've never seen before today. I'm being asked to bend over from the waist, bend over and spread my hands out on the cold metal while foreign hands ride up and down my sides, not quite reaching around for my soft spots, staying clear of those taboo places, frisking my sides, patting them officially, checking. I stand up. My first tendency is to laugh. "You've got to be kidding. This is a little play you need to rehearse. I just happened to come along—a female lead."

I should backtrack a bit here, in all fairness to Officer Littlefield, and say I was speeding. But you should know I was a pre–55-miles-per-hour teenager who grew up in Nevada with no posted speed limits on the open highways. I could drive out on those highways at a comfortable 85 miles per hour and be standing still when silver Porsches and high-finned Cadillacs passed me—120 miles per hour easy, no joke. As I told you, I've always tried to be truthful, tried to mend white lies that just popped out of my mouth before I had a chance to catch them.

So, I'm speeding north across the Navajo Reservation where I've never seen a patrol car. A niggling brain wave reminds me to slow down when I reach the border. Small Utah towns on Highway 89 make their yearly revenue on speeders. I don't listen. I want to get back to Salt Lake City. The sun's slipping into low gear in the wintry sky, and I'm ready to rest my head on a pillow.

Across the border and closing in on Panguitch, an old Mormon settlement, I'm rounding corners like I'm driving the Indy 500. I'm driving a car for our family friend, Thomas, who owns a car rental agency. He's just closed his office in Tucson and needs to have his inventory moved back to Salt Lake. Early this morning after my husband left us together at breakfast in the Sheraton Conquistador, I told Thomas, "Sure, let me take one of your cars back for you."

My until-death-do-we-partner, Daniel, planned dusk-to-dawn meetings on this, the last day of our vacation. He left me at the breakfast table like a cold pancake on a blue plate and didn't seem to care about the temptation he was exposing me to—our mutual friend, Thomas, who touches my leg sometimes under the table. I promised to be faithful. I try to keep my word.

After two hours' worth of an on-the-road, antispouse litany that has finally run its course, I've decided to enjoy this moment, this compact Plymouth Reliant, the panorama of red soil, skeletal sage, and bare-branched trees of early winter. Besides, I'm helping someone today; I'm a friend! "Yes," I tell myself, "it still counts to do nice things for people sometimes. There's a future for me in the credit column of life."

I'm congratulating myself, almost forgetting my poison-pen letter on the note pad in Room 237 of the Conquistador—*Dear Daniel . . .*—I see a Highway Patrolman parked on the opposite side of the road, colored lights flashing across the top of his white Dodge. Red, white, and blue. My flag. My country. And the Highway Patrolman is stabbing a long, muscular arm out of his window. His knife-blade finger directs me to pull over. He whips his car into a quick U-turn and pulls up behind me, a great big trooper with pro-forma mirrored sunglasses. He unfolds out of his white car, reeking with perverse satisfaction. He's caught a big fish—$$ for Garfield County. His lights whirl like crazy. He pats the top of his broad-brimmed hat and adjusts the under-the-occiput strap.

I deserve this. I step out into the wind and lean against the door, my arms folded.

"Good afternoon, officer." I look cool in the reflection of his sunglasses.

"You know you were going seventy-six miles per hour, Ma'am?"

"Yes, I do, sir." I assess him peripherally. I could be attracted to this lean, blond officer, his solid body, his height. I could wear high heels and still be short. He has a blond moustache, slightly outdated with its waxed tips, but nonetheless intriguing the way it accentuates his lips.

"Why were you going that fast, ma'am? You know it's against the law?"

I resist the temptation to lift his sunglasss from the bridge of his nose to see what might be possible in his eyes. Only a few hours away from this morning. New impulses already.

"You're absolutely right, sir. It's hard to drive this monotonous desert, these endless stretches. I'm anxious to get home to my family."

"It's unsafe at that speed, ma'am."

The wind is intruding on my bones. I'm getting testy. I want to tell him to forget the goody-two-shoes act and lay off the preaching. Do I need to hear one hundred reasons why I am a bad person?

"I'll have to cite you, ma'am."

Any thoughts of compromise on the high desert have flown with the gusty wind. He takes himself too seriously. I sink into my bucket seat, fold my legs back into the compact car, and slam the door against the wind. Luckily, I have a book, *How to Create Yourself,* but before I can finish a page, Office Littlefield is back, tapping at my window.

I roll it down slightly to keep the wind from blowing into my sensitive pink ears.

"I need to see your car registration."

I lean over to look in the jockey box, pull down sun visors, feel under the front seat. "I guess I don't have any. But I'm driving this car back to Salt Lake City for a friend who owns a rental car agency. I'm sure everything's in order."

"I'll call it in."

I roll up my window and rest my book on the steering wheel. I knot my forehead, hoping that extra concentration will help me forget this fiasco. True salvation. If possible. The creative process. A poetic interpretation of life with the chance to color or reinterpret, to replay, to recast any given scene. But then there is a flash of unnatural light. I look up to see another patrol car pulling in front of mine, the sunlight jagged like lightning across the clean windshield. My door is being opened by Officer Littlefield, who has a gun in his hand.

"Out of the car," he orders, poised like a stalking cat. "You're under arrest for possession of a stolen vehicle." He's stern, every move efficient.

My eyes might be as big as kiwi fruits, my wide-open mouth a watermelon. Neither of them will close. I obey. Never having been at gunpoint before except on the other side of a movie screen, I respect the metal, the trigger, the finger in the guard. I bend over, hands on the trunk of my car, while a green pickup truck carrying a mother with a young child on her lap slows to five miles per hour. The mother and the child stare at me, their eyes like four large dots on a white page, staring blankly and unforgivingly at my bent body and the gun held high in the air.

"We'll have to handcuff you," Officer Littlefield says. His voice is sure, if a little higher than before, squeezed tight by the alert muscles in his neck.

I know that I've done nothing wrong as I put my hands out in front of me compliantly, my two hands that have rocked babies, threaded needles, and stroked my husband's back. Ah yes, my husband. Daniel. His business meetings. Chalkboards. Flow charts. Progress reports. Sometimes I catch a glimpse of my name on his list of "Things to Do."

I stay with the logic here. I've seen enough movies and read enough articles about patrolmen getting their heads blown off, so

I'm cool. I'm above this situation, above crime, above it all. Except why am I standing here on Highway 89 in handcuffs, the wind swirling around my feet and up under my sweatshirt that reads "U.S.A." across the front?

Officer Littlefield says he will fasten my seat belt. He opens the door for me like a true gentleman, and, against my will, little edges of me are reverberating like they used to do on first dates. He says the handcuffs are for my protection as well as his. He is courtly, a Sir Walter Raleigh, saving me from myself. I follow his direction and don't stop to ask from what the cuffs are protecting me.

When Officer Littlefield launches into the Miranda Warning that I've heard a thousand times on police sitcoms, I suggest he doesn't need to, but he insists. ". . . And having these rights in mind, do you wish to talk to us now?"

"I'm returning this car for a friend who is closing out a car rental agency. I don't know anything more than that."

Before he shifts his big Dodge into drive, he pushes the button on his two-way radio and reads his mileage to the dispatcher. "Twenty-five, eight fifty-four. Am proceeding with suspect north on 89. Officer Cram's wife is riding with us to monitor the prisoner. Officer Cram is bringing in the stolen vehicle." Static on the radio, muffled dispatch words, static in my head.

The questions begin. "What if Thomas is in deep financial trouble, stealing cars to rev up his inventory? Can you trust a man who plays with your knee and thigh under the table at a restaurant while your husband is discussing the Dow-Jones? What if I'm being framed? My husband and Thomas together, fed up with me. Maybe I walked in my sleep and stole this car and haven't found out about it yet."

"Care for a smoke?" the officer asks. I don't smoke, but start to wonder if I should play the part of the criminal now—a broad, a cigarette hanging from the cliché corner of my mouth. Maybe I should think tough, too. *Hey, baby, aren't guns symbols for the manliness you don't feel inside?* My mind ranges through the dark interiors of tenement apartments in the darker interiors of movie houses. This is a movie. I'm not in Patrolman Littlefield's presence with handcuffs on my wrists. I'm not fastened under his car's seat belts;

I'm an actress riding north on Highway 89 in southern Utah, Garfield County, while the cameras roll.

"We'll bring the prisoner around to the back," Littlefield says over his radio. "Officer Cram, you park the stolen vehicle in front of the jailhouse." Then, Littlefield reads his mileage numbers to the dispatcher again.

"Why did you do that?" I ask.

"What?"

"The mileage?"

"Oh," Littlefield grins, "female prisoners. Sometimes, they claim they've been molested and raped, that kind of stuff. We keep things clean here in Garfield County."

Littlefield is bizarre, unreal, a combo of Mr. Clean and a cartoon Canadian Mountie. I'm uneasy. I only believe in fumbling, inconsistent humanity like Thomas, his fingertip circling on the palm of my hand under the table, and like me, my hand open and receptive. Dismiss this Littlefield.

A crowd has gathered at the back of the concrete building to watch the procession of the "Big Arrest of the Day," maybe of the year, for all I know, I feel like a zoo-person, bars painted across my body, black rings under my eyes, that hungry look of the damned etching itself into my face already. "Bless the beasts and the children," I hum as I pass the cork-eared and bee-eyed. Escorted and handcuffed, this is me climbing up hard concrete steps, walking into the arms of justice, wide open and ready to embrace me.

The admitting officer does have an ample bosom, but no open arms. Of those I encounter on this late winter afternoon, she believes me least of all. She asks for my earrings and my wedding ring and drops them into a three-by-five manila envelope. She doesn't respond at all while I'm posing for front and side mug shots and saying I've done nothing wrong and that I work with the Utah Alliance for the Hungry. She's like a sheet of rubber on her skin and in her heart.

The admitting officer calls in a patrolman—the official fingerprinter. He opens a metal box and presses my fingerpads into black ink, an exercise not unlike fingerpainting in kindergarten. He dips my ten little Indians into that ink pad one at a time. The prints look nothing like fingers should. They are fat, smudged twice their size, and spread out on a sectioned piece of paper on the desk. He asks me where I got the hole in my right thumbprint. I tell him that I quilt. I look over at the admitting officer, hoping for some response to that hint of domesticity. I wouldn't have thought criminals knew how to quilt, at least I never thought so until now, but then who ever thought I'd end up in the Garfield County Jail with somebody handing me a bright orange jumpsuit and telling me to remove everything except my bra and underpants.

The admitting officer stuffs this orange jumpsuit into my hands and tells me to change. I follow her like she's a sales clerk at a department store. I step inside my dressing room—a narrow cell with one limp mattress on a built-in shelf and one tinny toilet, the seat ring just large enough for a ten-year-old. I fold my sweatpants and sweatshirt neatly, as carefully as I can to prove I'm a well-ordered person and that my mother taught me right. I step into the legs of this orange jumpsuit, pull it up over my hips, zip it into place. Who else has zipped this ill-fitting suit around their hips and chest?

"I'm innocent," I tell the admitting officer who has her hands outstretched to receive my pile of possessions, the last vestige of the public me, and to lock it into a metal locker.

"Do you really believe that?" She closes the door between us. It locks into place heavily, separating me from a woman who might have liked me yesterday, who might have swapped pleasantries or beauty secrets. I'm waiting behind a door that has no knob on the inside. My new home.

I try sitting on the thin pallet, but the cell is cold, colder than the outside where the wind is blowing and whistling the November sun out of sight. I pace, shut away from everything in the world by that door that is locked and has no handle on the inside.

I shake it.

"What do you want?" The admitting officer's voice is humorless, irritated.

"When can I make my phone call?"

"What?" she yells.

"My phone call." I yell too.

"In a few minutes."

No faces at the door. Nobody in sight. Just voices echoing from other rooms where the dispatcher and several patrolmen are laughing and carrying on business as usual. The orange of the jumpsuit is seeping into my skin—Agent Orange, pumpkins rotting after Halloween, a bright spotlight to protect the hunted from dark places.

I volunteered to help Thomas this morning. A good impulse. An offering with an added twist I never expected, but I said I'd help him first. I wrote a screaming note to Daniel, but he needs to hear screams. He doesn't hear anything.

The remembrance of a needle is hard between my thumb and forefinger as I poke minuscule stitches into ghost calico. The feel of bread dough squeezes through my fingers. The heels of my hands push the lump back and forth on the floured breadboard. A baby curves into my neck. My hand strokes its softness like my hand stroked Thomas's curly black hair after he gave me the car key and said good-bye. Then, in that sun-bleached hotel room, I screamed a note to Daniel.

I don't like this narrow cell, the door that looks heavier every time I see it. I try to resurrect guidance from calendars and cure-yourself psychology books of my past. "Stay in the present moment. Experience the experience. Turn into the pain. Someday this will be funny. . . ." The words sound like flatulence from a tired old man in a nursing home. I don't like it here. For the first time since I saw the flashing red light on the patrol car, I face facts. I'm in jail, arrested for a federal offense. I want my mother. I want my innocence back.

I walk to the door, the one movable part of my cage. "Please, can I make my phone call?" My voice is strong and clear. I don't want them to know I'm folding into ten thousand creases where I can hide from everybody, slip under this door and the outer door, slip into freedom where I can speed down the highway of my life.

"Just a minute." The admitting officer sounds bored, like maybe she's yawning.

"You're supposed to let me make a phone call. I can clear things."

Keys rattle. I press my forehead to the cold metal door, and I'm back in a movie again except, of course, for the reality of my innocence. "I am innocent," I repeat to myself as I walk through the corridor with posture that my father used to say looked regal.

The office is small—two desks in one room, a glassed-in window behind which the dispatcher sits with her cup of coffee and radio equipment, another small office for the chief, I guess. Littlefield tells me where to sit, and the two other officers in the room look at me shyly for a minute before their eyes shift to their shoelaces. They want to believe me, I can tell. They know who I am, but they defer to Littlefield.

"I called Tucson a few minutes ago," Littlefield says. "Nobody knows anything yet, and most of the detectives have gone home for the night."

Who would I call even if my husband were home? Certainly not him after this morning. I don't want to call my children or alarm the babysitter. What if there's no one to answer my one phone call? Littlefield dials the number that I've written on a piece of notepaper.

"Good luck," he says, handing me the phone.

"Fox, McQuaid, and Chase," the receptionist says on the other end of the line. My best friend. Maybe she can help.

"Is Simpson there?"

"Yes, she is. May I say who's calling?"

"Oh, it's me, it's me," I say, elated.

"Who's calling, please?"

"I'm in jail. I need to talk to Simpson."

"One moment, please."

I don't want this to happen, I don't, really don't, but as I wait for her to answer the phone, my Adam's apple starts to quiver. I don't want to cry, not here, not in front of these highway patrolmen who haven't believed me like they should. I don't want to waste any emotion in this shabby office.

"Ma'am," the receptionist says in my ear, "I can't find her. I thought she was here."

"But I need her."

"Sorry. Will you hold, please?"

The handset is in my hand in the air, halfway between my ear and the cradle. It looks like a warped barbell, two weights on each end, Ma Bell's sagging bosom. The receiver is making noises. I look into the earpiece at the wait-on-hold music and think of doilies, tinfoil hearts, and spots of oozing glue, the creations I used to make with my children in February.

The receptionist is back and starts to ask what she can do to help when she has another call. The lavender music assaults my ear again. I take hold of the handset with two hands like I'm steering one of those bumper cars at the carnival and place it gently back into its cradle, where it rocks.

"Let's try the car rental agency in Salt Lake City," I say.

Patrolman Littlefield dials 1-411, listens, and dials again, He hands me the phone. A recording says the phone has been disconnected. When that clicks off, a loud dial tone blasts my ear.

"Anybody else?" he asks, tapping his pencil against his fingernails, one at a time, a scientific approach to pencil tapping.

"I could call my sister or even my mother. No, not my mother. She gets upset too easily. My sister. Try my sister." I write the phone number on a piece of paper. The officer dials and hands me the phone again. It rings and rings. I swallow. There is too much silence in the world I once imagined I lived in. All I can hear are mechanical responses to my innocence: clicks, tones, hums, buzzes, sloppy home-made valentine music in my ear. All I can see are hard surfaces: machines, pistols in holsters, badges over hearts, metallic eyes, keys that rattle, a belt buckle binding a soft belly.

"Should we try your mother?" Littlefield asks. He is becoming larger as he sits at the desk, tapping his pencil on each fingernail. He is ballooning up in his chair, his chest a steely righteousness. His teeth glow. Phosphorescent light. His moustache quivers with legality. I am shrinking in my chair, dressed in an orange jumpsuit without my wedding ring to twist around on my finger. The orange fabric is rubbing against my skin, its polyester fibers sticking me like prickly cactus. The phone is growing larger, ballooning away from me. Ma Bell's bosom further from my reach.

"My mother. I can't call her. She's frail, old, her bones are almost powder. The babysitter. I guess it will have to be the babysitter."

"If this call doesn't go through, we're going to have to put you back in the cell for a while. We've got other business."

The babysitter hears my voice. "Am I glad you called," she says. "Your Stephen has been cutting classes and the high school has been calling here. Your other son took off and didn't tell me where he was going. How can you expect me to do a good job for you if you don't discipline your children? When are you getting home, anyway?''

''I've been detained,'' I say, my skin puckering into folds as I shrink further into my chair. ''I just called to say that I'll be home a bit later than planned.''

''Well, that's real fine. You promised me . . .''

''Daniel will be flying home tonight sometime, I don't know when. He'll pay you extra.''

''I certainly hope so. What's happened to your children? They used to be nice.''

''Good-bye.''

The array of patrolmen is impressive. They are tall, mostly in good physical condition except for one hanging belly. They are not looking at me in the right way. There is not enough respect. Littlefield's fingers squeeze around my biceps and curl into the muscle. He is still growing, subtly filling with his surety and firm conviction that he is protecting society. He is steady as he leads me back to the cell, back to the grey that is now the murky color of near night.

Officer Littlefield is a bit quaint, even gallant. A Clark Gable, a John Wayne. He is strong by my side. I like his strength, the fact that he is bigger than I am. And his eyes. I didn't see them in the beginning because of the mirrors painted onto his sunglasses. But now his eyes, his pale blue eyes tinted with a desert loneliness, can see into me. He escorts me to my cell, my apartment; he asks no favors; he says, ''Good night, sleep tight.''

And I am alone, failures flapping like the end of a reel of film in my mind. It is useless to call anyone else. My time has come. Maybe, deep down, even though I wanted to believe in a merciful, poetic, flexible God, a screenwriter or a novelist who can rewrite when a situation starts to overwhelm the protagonist, the truth is, my time has come. I knew it would happen sooner or later. I always knew about the underside of my heart, that it could be seen by someone with eyes to see, someone who bothered to focus long enough, someone who was not too busy to look my way. I sink to the hardness of my bed. There are no springs to squeak. I curl up on a plywood cupboard, a shelf for those who need to be stored away.

And I smile for the world that has held me together—my quilts, my friends, my family—that now has as much substance as talc. I celebrate the people's good fortune in having barriers like receptionists and business meetings to protect them from me, the woman with the defective soul who has hidden it between quilt blocks and between slices of honey whole-wheat bread. I've played a royal Let's Pretend. My children are paper dolls I cut from a Sprouse Reitz book, the one I bought for twenty-nine cents with money I stole from my best friend when I was eight years old.

The quilting, the needles. Imaginative thread, lacing through my eyes, needles poking the beliefs I have lived by. One, two, buckle my shoe. I bend over to retie my laces. Why did I buy these running shoes? I should have known I couldn't keep running. Here I am. They've caught me.

I long for Littlefield to come back. He's the only sure thing I know. There is no comfort in grey walls, grey areas that are half light/half dark, half tones, and, ultimately, the hollow inside of the whole.

And a vision wells up in front of me, in front of those bars and the grey: a spinning ball of white light, its edges trembling with power. The light dazzles me. I shield my eyes. I'm mesmerized by this light of the law. It unclothes me. As the light lifts the burden of pretense from my shoulders, I watch it hover. Suddenly I know I don't have to try anymore. No more need to make up stories. The weight has been lifted. I am free.

Radio KENO

Chloe was just far enough from Las Vegas to see its lights competing with each other, even in broad daylight. A twenty-four hour peep show. A movie set with one-sided buildings. The closer she drove to the city and to Wagner, the more unreal everything seemed—pale purple mountains rising from the valley floor like cardboard props, the backdrop of blank blue.

She pressed the scanner. The station had been in the 90s, specifically 98.6. Radio KENO—the spot on the dial reserved for her and Wagner. She caught a synthesized drumbeat on the old frequency, but there were no hormones in this new music. Nothing to start the grinding inside.

Chloe dropped her jaw slack and let the words roll up out of her. "Wagner," she said in slow time. "He loves me. He loves me not."

The car halted in the middle of the highway while the bushes and sand raced past. The yellow lines streamed under the front of her hood, the purple mountains blurred. Her car stood still, motionless, until suddenly the scenery stopped and a Chevron station appeared.

Chloe stepped out of her sleek car, the wind ragging her shirt, and dropped a quarter in the pay phone. "I'm in town," she said.

The people of Wagner's street tended their lawns, mended the links in their fences, and cultivated borders of cactus and rocks. She drove slowly, the numbers growing larger. 1997. 2001. She thought of Wagner pressing close to her in his car on the hill above this city and its lights. Tongues sliding past lips, the surface of teeth extraordinary. Fingers searching for accelerated pulses. And Chloe tracing Wagner's collar bone with her two fingers, slipping off the ridge, sliding deeper into his territory until she remembered the picture of the sad-eyed Jesus on her wall. His gathers of white muslin. His long brown hair backlit with ocher light.

"I love you," he'd begged as she bent out of reach.

"I'm saving myself," she'd said.

Savings in a bank, gathering interest. Money to pay Jesus and Father at The Gate. Chloe pounded the steering wheel slowly with the side of her fist.

2005. The pink paint and mauve shutters had their bare spots. She felt perspiration under her belt and a moistness in the wrinkles of her cotton duck pants. She breathed deeply.

Wagner's driveway felt hard under her feet. She'd heard he worked in concrete now and wore his hair in a ponytail. Undoubtedly, he'd poured this cement. She put one foot forward, the other ahead of that, but moved nowhere. The grass and a bed of yellow marigolds drifted by as Chloe walked, yet the house and her car stayed equidistant from her place on the sidewalk.

Their song was "Happy, Happy Birthday, Baby." She'd dedicated it to him on KENO the night before she went away, bailed out, ran from him in her crinoline slip—her parachute. She fell through fog and clouds, trying to see Jesus' face, falling, falling away for Jesus. And with the mist clinging to her ankles and arms, she found an upright man with Jesus on his lips. They landed into marriage as if they were puffs of white cotton falling to the ground, no hard edge.

Here she was, on Wagner's driveway, treading concrete, trying to find solidity, a foothold, yet the surface pitched and rolled. But then Wagner came out of the house. His hair was twenty years thinner. A limp ponytail brushed the tip of a shoulder blade. Stark nose. Impassive cheeks. An inscrutable, pinched face.

She looked for signals, hoping his eyes would cut straight through as before. She thought she saw desire at the corner of his mouth, running for safety in the desert beige of his cheek. His eyes focused just to the side of her face while the water from the lawn sprinkler rippled and warped like seaweed in an undercurrent. The grass and marigolds swayed. Chloe thought of swimming to the surface for air, but adjusted her footing instead. A wider stance.

"It's Chloe," he said, looking over the top of her head, the grass and the marigolds stiff.

He shook her hand, and everything turned liquid and filled with floating white petals. Chloe plucked one to hold. *He loves me.*

The screen door bounced twice against its frame.

"You remember Shauna, don't you?" he said. His wife stood in an archway. She was a peaceful woman, though as a girl she'd shadowed Wagner in high school, waiting for Chloe to disappear.

"Yes. Shauna," Chloe said. "Yes. Nice to see you."

"You've barely changed," Shauna said.

"It's been a long time." Chloe followed them inside. "I needed to touch base."

She walked to the easy chair, tried to sit down, but the chair eluded her. She straightened to rebalance, then noticed an amateurishly painted mural on the wall—a picture of a Christian-book-cover blonde with Mrs. America cheekbones. Solid. Strong in her convictions. Her outstretched hands placating the animals surrounding her. A shepherdess. Chloe steadied her eyes on Wagner to help her find her way into the chair. He was the only stillness.

His narrow face. The same. Some people had called him mean. The eyes had a cutting edge. Her friends called him thoughtless, somebody who didn't care. If she hadn't known about souls, she might have believed them. But she'd seen his soul on his bed behind venetian blinds when no one else was there. They'd searched each other's bodies for soft places to mesh and blend. Jesus, the chastity belt, had smiled at them peacefully while they fumbled, touched palms, stroked surfaces. Chloe would never break her vow. She had told Wagner she'd hate him if she did.

"Sit down," he said. "May we get you something? Water, juice?" Even though he had muscled arms, he was emaciated in a vegetarian sort of way. Calm.

"Water is fine."

Shauna went to the kitchen and returned holding a gigantic mug with words printed on its side: *Whosoever drinketh of this water shall thirst again.*

"So is there something wrong with the water at this house?" Chloe asked, laughing a little, swirling the ice cubes.

"What do you do?" Wagner asked.

"Oh," Chloe shrugged, "A little of this and that, children, PTA, you know, the usual. By the way, that's an interesting mural on your wall."

The shepherdess dressed in white was painted with globs of oil, spackled thick like cake frosting. She was walking toward a mountain. Behind trees and rocks, bears, raccoons, and field mice watched her. She was suspended, her legs unable to move without a new brush stroke.

"A friend painted it for us," Shauna said proudly.

"I know this is a cliché," Wagner said to Chloe, "but are you happy?"

She looked at her fingernails, then over at the worn sofa that had stains from dogs, cats, children's popsicles. "Of course. And you?"

"We've found Christ," Shauna answered for him.

"Funny thing," Chloe said. "Is that true, Wagner?"

"Hey, remember Bobby Elsner?" Wagner asked. "He's dealing blackjack over at the Nugget now." The inset of blue mesh in his nylon tank top displayed his shoulders. He must have tossed thousands of bags of cement.

Shauna put her arm around Wagner's shoulders. "Wagner's not quite as sure as I am, but close."

"A matter of inches, Wagner?" Chloe avoided Shauna's pleasant face, which she feared might light up. She crossed her legs at the knee, realized she was slumping into the chair, and sat up tall.

"We try," Shauna said calmly.

Chloe shifted her attention to a pair of roller skates coupled haphazardly in the corner. Then she looked more closely at the details in the mural. A rainbow, lines of gold glitter separating each stripe, jutted from the depths of the ecumenical forest where parrots and leopards, musk oxen and emus peeked through big-leafed foliage. A longhorn beetle hid under a leaf, one elongated antenna out, one golden eye surveying the path to the mountain. The shepherdess seemed unconcerned about the melange of creatures or the time it was taking her to get to the mountain. Chloe's eyes wandered from the mural to the boxes of toys in the corners. Pots of seedlings. Macrame plant holders.

Children argued in the backyard. Wagner left the room, and Chloe heard the squeaking of a screen door. "Calm down out there," he said as if he were saying good morning to a friend.

She tried not to stare at Wagner, but she wanted nothing more than a long, clean look. Was there a clue in his eyes? Something he'd forgotten to say? Why hadn't he stood up to Jesus if he loved her? She could feel him seeping into her skin again—his nonchalant way of letting life come to him, no hands on his clock, no wild swings of his pendulum.

"Our children go to gymnastics twice a week," Shauna was saying.

"They must be good," Chloe said, wishing for an eclipse of Shauna's light. And she wished she could breathe. There was so much humidity in the air.

The pitch of argument from the backyard grew louder until a small girl rushed into the room. "He took my ball!"

"No, I didn't." Her brother blasted in behind her. "Indian giver!"

"No, I'm not." She punched him in the jaw.

"Kelly. Alexis," Shauna said, patiently wiping mud from her daughter's cheek while her other hand stayed Kelly. "Daddy's old friend is here today. Are you two going to act like this for his friend?"

"Daddy doesn't have any friends." Alexis pulled both sides of her mouth with her fingers and stuck her tongue out at everything in the room.

"Friends," said Chloe, amused. "You don't believe in friends, Alexis?"

"You're stupid!"

Shauna put her finger across Alexis' lips. "Shhh."

Alexis punched the air in Chloe's direction.

"So," Shauna said as her daughter climbed onto her lap and burrowed tight against her breast. But then, Kelly charged, head first.

"You stupid stupid," Alexis screamed.

"Shauna, for hell's sake," said Wagner.

Shauna laughed as if amused by the unthinkable ways of children. She hooked her hands into both shirt collars and scooted the two children out of the room while they hit at each other and called names.

"Boring, isn't it?" Chloe said to Wagner, sipping water from her mug.

Wagner stacked his hands into a meditative position, closed his eyes, and leaned back into the cushion. "Why did you come?"

"Old times. Can't erase it, blotto . . . you know?"

"You want to know if you're forgiven, don't you?" he said.

"Forgiven?"

"You know what I mean."

Shauna came back, rebuttoning the cuffs of her blouse. "Please excuse the children, Chloe. Some days . . ."

Alexis trailed through the living room with a blanket draped around her like a toga. She twirled a few times and fell into her mother's lap. Chloe watched mother and child kiss each other's cheeks and hated herself for sitting there like a high priestess looking for her lost court. But she'd been driven by her car across mountains and deserts to Wagner's front door. She couldn't help it. Maybe she could walk into the mural and head for the mountains. Or maybe she could get back to the driveway. But what if he didn't follow her? What if he didn't say, *You still matter?*

"Tell us about your family," Shauna said.

"My husband is a nice man, but he's lost somewhere in the middle of his niceness."

Shauna seemed startled.

"It's okay. We've worked things out. A few compromises." Chloe sighed, the woman who, as a girl, had thought she could stop the sun from disappearing at night or push a windstorm backward with her hands if she only had enough faith. "And I have two teenage daughters. The joy of motherhood is elusive, however."

"Careful how you speak," Shauna said. "They'll act how you expect them to act."

"They weary me. I shouldn't have been a mother or a wife." *I should never have left Wagner.*

Shauna rose from her chair. "I have something that might help you," she said, her pink floral blouse pulsing like a garden. "We've got to keep seeking for the answers, we've got to make this world a better place."

"Why?" Chloe asked.

"We could blow ourselves up."

"Why postpone things?"

"You don't mean that," Shauna said as she disappeared down the hall.

Chloe laughed nervously. "Don't mind me, Wagner. Good old cynicism. Harbor for the wounded."

Wagner sat small in the cushions, hunched over, contemplating. "This is hard on my family."

"Well, you always did let everyone else cover your bets."

He sat still. "Why are you so bitter? Aren't you happy with your choice?"

"I don't believe in love," said Chloe, "and probably not in God. Stories to keep people in the chutes. You never loved me."

"On the contrary," he said simply. "You never loved me. Always looking for white robes and light."

"You just let me go off, babbling about Jesus."

"It's funny how Shauna took up your cause." Wagner changed position, crossed the other leg, and slowly traced his upper lip with one finger. "I married *you* after all. So what happened to the sacred vessel?"

"I can't stand still."

"You never could." Wagner looked straight into her eyes, the way he used to. She held her breath until she lost her gravity, the chair rocked, the carpet rolled up and back across the room. Wagner didn't flinch. His eyes bored into Chloe's, sawed right through the cornea. Tools for eyes. They could have jackhammered Chloe into broken concrete except that Shauna returned and placed a book in Chloe's lap: *You Never Have to Have Another Bad Day.* She patted Chloe's arm, sunlight pouring from her hands.

As Chloe smiled at her, Wagner's wife's fingers slid down to her hand. "It's good you came by," she said. "It's nice to see old friends."

Chloe filtered Shauna's words to estimate their content. With her free hand, she pulled the hem of her pants over her calves. *It's just a little thing I want. To know if he still loves me.* She coughed to expel compressed emotion, but it spun through her head and the room began to turn. The girl on the wall winked. "Come with me," she gestured.

No. Chloe squeezed her kneecap to keep her senses.

"You're shaking, Chloe." Shauna knelt by her side and sandwiched Chloe's hand.

"It's the change in altitude." Chloe felt her axis slipping further, everything askew, the wall tipping.

Not bodies. Chloe, the shepherdess said. *They go away. Gravity grabs for your thighs and the flesh sags.* The fair-haired painting stretched her arms further out of the wall; her dress billowed.

If only Chloe could run to Wagner and throw herself over him like a wool blanket, she could save him. But the animals began to growl. They padded out of the wall onto the shag carpet—a rhinoceros that Chloe hadn't noticed before, one of the bears, a mandrill, a tiger. A parrot flew out of dense foliage. The wall shook, and the shepherdess shouted.

Chloe tried to hear if Wagner might be whispering to her—"You'll never know how many times I've wanted you back." She looked for traces in his eyes, while a tiger stalked her heel and the rhino sniffed her shoe.

The woman on the wall was hysterical.

The tiger pawed the carpet, sharpening its claws. Chloe smelled the rhino's river-bottom breath as its jaws came close to her face.

"Shauna, your hand is hot," Chloe said. "It's giving me a fever."

"What's wrong, Chloe?" Wagner said passively. He was a statue. "Can I get you some more water to drink?"

"Chloe," she pleaded for him to say. If only he'd jump up and take charge: say, "Stop everything," pull his belt from its loops in his pants, and lash the animals back to the wall. He'd lash until every animal, even the birds, returned to its lair. He'd shove the rhino back into that painted water.

And afterwards, she'd have that to remember.

Through the blur, Chloe saw the distinct figure of Kelly bouncing back into the room. "I've got to go," she said, pulling her hand back to herself.

"I'm glad," said Alexis.

"Alexis," said Shauna, grabbing her by the wrist. "She's our guest." But Shauna's voice didn't match her words. She lifted Alexis to the sofa and Wagner's side.

Suddenly, Wagner moved. Out of the foam and the springs and the upholstery fabric, he moved like an abruptly shifting glacier after centuries of imperceptible travel.

"Shauna," he said. Chloe could hear the forest pines crack. "Kelly. Alexis." Wagner stood, solitary. He looked down at each of them, slowly, deliberately.

"Do you know I used to kiss this woman?" He pointed to Chloe.

Alexis shrank into her mother's cleavage. Kelly looked confused. Shauna stroked the child's hair as if it were her own.

"In fact, Alexis," Wagner was saying, kneeling down to make eye contact and forcing Alexis's face toward his with his finger, "I used to drive her around in my car. We dedicated songs to each other on the radio. She could have been your mother."

"Oh, God in heaven," said Shauna. She tried to rise out of the upholstery with Alexis's clinging weight on top of her.

"No," said Wagner. "Sit right there."

"I didn't mean this to happen, Wagner," Chloe stammered. She stood up and stamped her feet to release her pant legs from their tight grip of her calves.

But when Wagner walked toward Chloe, the room leaned ninety degrees. He frightened her as he reached for her shoulders and pulled her to him.

"Don't think you're getting off so easy," he said.

"Wagner?" Shauna's voice was hesitant.

Chloe tried to pull herself into her own folded arms, but Wagner's grip was firm. "Don't. I'm not really here."

"Wagner, you're not like this!" Shauna struggled off the sofa, lifting Alexis with her, her sunlight extinguished, the beam cut off from its source of light. She faced Chloe.

"He's hurting me in front of our children."

Wagner broke into the words. "Just listen!"

Shauna froze.

"This woman," Wagner pointed a long finger at Chloe, "was obsessed, just like you."

Chloe looked to the wall for deep foliage or elephant ear leaves under which to hide, but the golden eye of the longhorn beetle glowed, warning her away. The shepherdess turned her back and headed for the mountains. The rest of the animals were still.

"Don't ever use people, Alexis, Kelly. And, Shauna, enough Jesus from you."

"I'm leaving," Chloe said.

Wagner shifted suddenly, released Chloe, sat on the fat cushions, and retreated behind his eyes. Shauna picked up her book that had fallen to the floor. She tried to pat Chloe's wrist, but couldn't seem to find it.

"I'm asking you," Chloe whispered. "Can't you understand He's always around the next corner, haunting me, waiting for me? This isn't easy."

"What?" Wagner asked.

"He'll never leave me alone," she said.

"Who?"

Kelly revved across the room. "Lunchtime," he crowed.

"Go drive your cars in the yard, you little devil." Shauna picked him up and shoved him out the screen door. She locked it after she slammed it.

He pounded on the wire mesh. "I'm hungry. I want bologna and cheese and a boiled egg and . . ."

"Shut up," Shauna yelled, covering her ears. Dust came pouring out of everything from the clouds on the mural. Everyone stood still while it sifted slowly back in to place. The finest powder Chloe had ever seen drifted over the chairs, her blouse, the carpet.

The animals and seeker in the mural moved first, jointed toys tiptoeing on mechanical legs, walking further into the wall. Outside the screen door, Kelly's head cocked from side to side as if he were a paper doll with a metal grommet at his neck. He sang in a Pinocchio voice: "Lunchtime. Bologna." Alexis squeezed her mother's leg, opening and closing her grasp like a wooden clothespin with a spring. The petaled collar surrounding Shauna's face flapped mechanically.

Chloe took a last look at Wagner. He looked like the bronzed fortune-teller under glass at the carnival, twenty-five cents for one fortune.

"It's time," she said.

Shauna unlocked the screen door.

"See-you-la-ter," they all said together and waved windshield-wiper arms.

"Love-to-your-fam-lee." Shauna blew continuous kisses in between waves.

"Peace be with you," Chloe said.

"Good-bye," Wagner said.

They kept waving as Chloe got into her car and drove onto the conveyor-belt street. It jerked and squeaked and carried Chloe and her car with its blaring radio out of the city with the famous lights, away from the one-walled chapels of the West and the cardboard mountains.

Baby Birds

He's not made to be this color. Six foot two and a half. Brown eyes. Beautiful like a Greek statue. I'm frightened when he's grey, like right now by the kitchen window in the offbeat light of the moon.

When I'm in an airplane and first enter a cloud, I'm excited. I like the misty feeling for a while, but then I think, "Enough of this," and long for the shape of a cloud that looks like something—a turtle or a rabbit or a ceaselessly puffing balloon.

His borders are murky now. Water drips occasionally from the faucet onto my stainless-steel sink as I observe him being everywhere at the same time. He's sailing on wind currents, scratching the sky with his fingernails, and dragging his legs simultaneously. He's blurred. He's high.

"Where have you been this late?" His shoulders rise like shoulder pads and then deflate back into place. My son's profile usually matches the classical Greek silhouette on old coins, but when he puts the flats of his hands on the edges of the kitchen sink, throws his head back and lets it rest in that position, his face is a puddle of creamy moonlight and shadow.

"Your eyes don't look so good." They're glass marbles shining in the dark of this kitchen at three in the morning.

The shoulders shrug again.

"Glad you're home. Should I tuck you in? Maybe you'll wake up like you used to, babbling, singing nonsense, eager for breakfast."

I think of the baby birds. The ivy on the side of the house, torn away last month when we were repainting. The nest hidden in the ivy. The birds were only sparrows, but there they were. Three babies chirping, raising havoc for having been found and exposed to the light. Ugly little babies, actually. Big veined eyes stretched over a large portion of head, no feathers to soften their presence. Eyes and open mouths.

The painter started to stuff them in the garbage can with the ivy. ''No,'' Michael said with alarm. ''Don't do that. I'll take care of them.''

''What will you do with them?'' the painter asked. ''Do you know about baby sparrows?''

Michael found a blue shoe box with a stylized check mark slashed across its side and a bold ''Nike'' written against the white background. He gathered cotton balls, soft twigs, old newspapers, bits of thread, a handful of dirt, and set the old nest and the three birds inside the box.

''So, you've been at it again,'' I say. His eyes are murky and red behind their shining surfaces in the moonlight by the window in our kitchen. ''Why in the hell didn't you call me when you said you would?''

His head tilts to the side. Not a yes or a no or an answer.

''Wipe that stupid slippery smile off your face, you idiot!'' I'm screaming with an opulent rage that isn't really mine. It belongs to some madwoman part of myself who has escaped her cage and is screaming at this boy in front of me. ''When are you going to grow up or wise up or shape up or do whatever up is the right up? You're so stupid, you're so stupid,'' and I'm carrying on like some fishwife and wishing I'd had the self-discipline to stay in bed and read the novel that's been waiting for me. But the printed words blur when Michael isn't home in the middle of the night. Every space between paragraphs reminds me to worry. The novel becomes the Book of Michael according to the Late Night Worrier, me, this neurotic person I don't accept as me even though she has fully taken over my body.

''Why do you keep doing this?'' I want him to bleed, maybe. To hurt like I do when I see this warping.

He half sits, half leans against the kitchen sink. He folds his arms, part of his methodology for enduring lectures, and he looks at me from his greyness and isn't really there. Who am I talking to?

After he made the shoe box into a comfortable domicile, Michael called the owner of The Animal Den, a pet store we once frequented to buy gerbils, hamsters, canaries, parakeets. Because the sun had settled behind the mountains for the night, he called the owner at his home. ''Please. What can I do for these birds?''

He was usually shy on the phone, sometimes asked me to ask for him, but this time he dialed the number, interrupted the owner's TV show, and held to his purpose for calling.

''Dig some worms,'' the animal man told him. ''Cut them up very small. Feed them to the birds with plastic tweezers. Give them lots of water. Then come to my store in the morning. I'll give you some pellets they'll like.'' And Michael went out in the dark with a trowel. When he couldn't find enough worms in our yard, he asked the next-door neighbor, who's a fisherman, for help. He came home with eight succulent worms, a night's worth of survival, and minced them until they were edible.

The birds were noisy and demanding. Their chirping pierced through everything else in the house—phone conversations, people coming to call, dreams at night. They were hungry again right after they were fed, but Michael didn't care. He stayed with them through the night and slept by the blue Nike box.

''Look. They're getting stronger,'' he told me, his father, and his brother. ''They're filling out, at least two of them are.'' I could almost see the bigger birds improve with my naked eye, no time-lapse photography necessary. Little feathers curling out of them. Wispy bits of bird plumage coming to their rescue, giving them a better presentation. But the smallest one seemed determined to grow away from life. Thin, scrawny, finally unable to stand on his two wispy claws.

''How can you keep doing this?'' I'm still yelling at him, at least this stranger is yelling who lives in me and comes out at night to hate this son who messes with his mind and his head and his body. And all of a sudden, my barrage of words sounds so hollow and empty. My throat hurts, and Michael is standing in front of me like a hard shell off which my words bounce. Boomerang words jumping back to me, hurting my ears, my throat. And Michael turns his face to the moonlight and I see those eyes that shine like plastic eyes on store-bought dolls. ''Mama, Mama,'' the baby doll in me cries. ''Protect us.''

''There's a bird hitting itself against my window,'' Michael told me two days after he adopted the babies. ''Maybe it's their mother.''

"But I thought birds abandoned their young after they've been touched by humans."

"So did I," he said, "but come in my room and wait with me. You'll see it happen. Every so often, she flies against the glass."

I didn't have to wait long. Whenever the two remaining babies cried for food, what we thought must be the mother bashed against the window, sometimes the screen. She scratched at the glass, her claws like fingernails on a blackboard.

"She's going to hurt herself," I said. "I've never heard of this happening. This might be a story for *Audubon.*"

"Maybe we'll have to take them outside," Michael said, rather hesitant. After all, he'd adopted this small menagerie and set up house in earnest. But that afternoon, after he found that one of them had hopped out of the box and was scratching on the cover of an Iron Maiden album lying on his dresser, Michael came into the kitchen with the box and birds in his hands.

"Maybe I'd better teach them to fly," he said in a soft voice.

"How can you do that?" I asked.

"Maybe I can toss them a few inches at a time."

He rubbed the breast of one bird until it climbed onto his finger. The baby swayed for a minute like it might fall, but righted itself. Michael stroked its feathers that seemed to be multiplying like yeast in a warm room. Then he carried the babies out the door to a patch of grass in the front yard, and I followed a few steps behind. Sitting cross-legged in the grass, he held out his finger again, a perch for his apprentice.

"Your name is Max," he said, taking Max in hand, holding him a few inches from the grass where he couldn't get hurt if he fell. "Up you go," he said, barely tossing the fluff into the air. The wings were awkward, but not ineffectual. They fluttered, gained altitude for a few inches, and then Michael caught Max like soft cotton in his hands. He tossed the bird higher on the next round, and Max flew to a low, poking branch and landed against a spray of aspen leaves.

"Right on, Max," Michael shouted, then bent over the box again. "And you're Martha," he told the second one. She was slower, but not by much. Michael laughed and tossed his protégée a little higher. "Look, Ma, no hands."

Three tosses and Martha gained altitude, actually flew to a branch above her brother, and posed like a seasoned aviator.

And then we heard a piercing chirp from a tall elm in our neighbor's yard.

"I bet that's their mother," I said. "That's got to be her again."

Michael's babies were less than steady on the aspen branches. He walked a few feet from them. "Come on, Max and Martha," he said. "Fly to me." They didn't move, but just bounced up and down on the thinness of the twig.

"They're tired now." He scooped them into his hands and put them back into the shoe box, but this seemed only to energize the birds. They hopped up and down like fish in a frenzied feeding, little pistons bouncing up and down, but Michael tucked the box under his arm and carried them into the house. "They're not ready yet. Maybe tomorrow."

"You promised me, Michael!" I'm crying now. The screaming went on for long enough. My tactics change. "You keep promising me, and you keep breaking that promise. Why do you do this to me? Why do you do this to yourself?"

The tears are old. I've cried them before, and they feel recycled, less saline this time, but I can't stop. "I'm just a rope-a-dope, Michael. You keep punching me in the head, I keep crying, wanting my head to feel better, then I'm back in the ring again. Each of us throwing punches at the other, nobody winning, nobody losing except both of us."

Michael repeats the shoulders, a loose scarecrow patterned with shadows cast by the crossbars in the window. He's so big, yet he's so helpless, standing there, numb to everything, even himself, hearing me from the inside of a cloud. Stupor. Vapor.

"I don't mean to," he says. "It just happens. I can't go anywhere it isn't. Know what I mean?"

"You've got to get some new friends. How can you find new friends if you keep going to the same old places?"

"Sure, Mom. Just walk right out the door and there's a crowd waiting for me."

I retie the belt on my bathrobe, feeling the comfort of a firm loop at my waist. I find an empty glass on the cupboard that looks clean enough in this half light. The water. The sound of the running water in my stainless-steel sink. If it's so stainless, why are there always spots of water on this sink? I can wipe them away but they always come back in slightly different spots and shapes. Even when I use Ajax, the ghostly outline of water and where it has been never leaves even though I polish the surface with a terrycloth towel. They always come back, maybe because we use so much water at this sink. Water for drinking, for diluting grape juice, water for washing grated carrots off hands, water to whirl in the disposal. Disposal of the unusable. Skins of cucumbers, carrots, potatoes. Radish tops. Green onions.

Then I feel a shift in gears. A new phase.

"How do I love thee, Michael?" The poetic phase is coming. After the screaming and the crying, then the poetics, the philosophizing, the rationalizing, the appeasement of the hurt inside me and Michael. I hug myself with my uneasy arms, rock something in them, maybe only my breasts though it feels like it should be more than that. But I'm not ready to embrace him yet. To forgive or forget like so many other times.

Michael didn't want to take the birds outside the next day. I found him lying on his bed with the shoe box between his hands, gazing into the shallow rectangular nest he'd made for his birds. Max and Martha had decorated the box brown, little squiggles of digested matter embellishing the once clean cotton, newspaper, and string.

"Messy little guys, aren't they?" he said almost too quietly.

"Guys?" I asked.

"Well, who knows what they are? I don't know the difference. Max and Martha is as good a guess as any."

"I'm proud of you," I said, trying to measure my voice out in level teaspoonsful so he wouldn't be frightened by its unevenness. "You're a better mother than I am, I think."

He looked up at me and smiled his brilliant smile. My woodchuck rescued by the orthodontist. Tall. Lanky. "This is hard," he said. "I know they're going to fly away this time. I was hoping I could keep them. Grow up together, sort of." He tucked his knees under his reclined stomach and knelt in front of the box which was covered with a loosely woven cheesecloth to keep the birds from flying all over his room. "Hi, Max. Martha. Are you excited to go back outside?" He peeked under the cloth, slid his hand inside, and brought it out with both birds side by side on his finger.

"Two peas in a pod," I said. "You should have named them Max and Max." I sat on the edge of the bed and rubbed my son's back, a smooth hand sliding up and down his rippling backbone.

"It's time," he said, as he kissed the birds on their heads. They trusted him, it seemed. Gave their allegiance to his steady hand. I kissed Michael mid-back, and we both trudged down the hall rather slowly, neither of us anxious to say good-bye.

At first, they flew to their familiar aspen branches. Michael reached up and teased them back on his finger, then tossed them in the air again. Each time, a higher branch, a farther tree. Michael ran into the house for a chair. He lodged it next to the new tree they'd claimed, climbed onto the raffia seat, and reached up for Max's breast until he perched again on Michael's outstretched finger. Michael blew his feathers with soft air from his lips, and then tossed him up again.

The mother moved in closer, flying in from the gigantic elm to a wispier aspen, calling steadily to Max and Martha. And for just one minute, the sky seemed to widen and open up into a paler blue than before and pull Max and Martha and their mother into its vortex. Some unseen force vacuuming the sky. The tiny black specks dotted the blue for a brief moment and then disappeared.

We couldn't say anything just then, just watched for dots to speckle the horizon again or sounds of the sparrows to whisper to us.

"They'll come back and see me," Michael said. "I know they will."

The moonlight leaks through the leaves of the chestnut tree outside the window, fractionating the space between us.

"Mom," he says through the curling fog around his body, "I'm too tired right now."

"But I need to tell you how I love you," I say, trying to minimize the whine that creeps into my voice at times like this. "Why won't you listen to me? I need to let you know because I've just been yelling at you and accusing you and telling you you're an idiot. There's someone inside me who still loves you no matter what you do. You need to hear her, too."

"I'm too tired," he says and pulls at the sleeves of his Levi jacket with the ascending angel painted on the back.

"We've got to do something," I say. "I'll make some phone calls. Will you talk to the counselor again?"

"I don't need help."

"That's what you keep saying," I say, a hard edge limning my voice. "I want my son back. You're a stranger who's grey and confused and lost to me and everyone else."

"I'll stop. Tomorrow. Let me sleep."

And I'm outside pecking at the glass of his eyes. "No, baby. You can't sweep me under the rug with everything else."

I'll find him, I promise myself. Tomorrow. I'll call somebody new. I'll read more books. I'll find a way.

"Leave me alone," he says, sliding out of his Levi jacket and down the shadowed channel of stairs.

"I wish I could," I say all the way to my bed and the forgetting that waits for me.

Anne at the Shore

DAY TWO

The day is at half point. Anne walks along the sand, the water curling over her toes. She makes prints—her five toes, the ball, arch, and heel of each foot.

The air is crowded. Anne can hear the beating of wings in the air, thousands of wings—small birds, birds of prey, birds that no longer live, possibly angels. Wings beating the air, chopping it into pieces. She would count the wings if the sea would ever be quiet, but water will have its way. Water filling her eyes; water rising in the air. Anne breathes water mixed with wind that whips her hair around her oval face.

Out of this compromised air, a man appears carrying a bulky burlap bag. He wears a red-and-black-checked shirt and shoeshine-black pants. The sun hovers between morning and afternoon as Anne walks past the man, wondering what he carries in his bag. Dry spots circle each of their footsteps, the weight of each step erasing wetness from the sand.

Kites dart through the wind—dragons, hawks, seagulls, twisters. Below the kites, the figure of a woman lies in the sand. Anne looks for movement under the cover of sand. She approaches the dormant figure, an Egyptian sarcophagus, passive, conceptually dead. The woman's eyes are open, her nose definite. Hair swirls around her head as if she were under water, the currents combing the strands. Her mouth is open in anticipation of conversation.

Anne kneels by her side and traces the insides of the sculpted legs. They are not proportioned to the rest of the body, but are half their expected length. They disappear into the sand below the knees.

"Her legs are funny." A little girl in a yellow-and-white-checked sunsuit carrying a blue pail squeezes her eyebrows together and then demands of Anne. "Why?"

"Someone ran out of time, maybe."

"She's not like my doll." The girl walks away toward the water, sits suddenly, and digs with her shovel.

The figure's breasts are half formed, barely suggested on her chest. A sculptor promised life to this woman, but abandoned her too soon. A bas-relief woman.

Above, seagulls coast. Below, a crow tracks the sand, transporting a protesting sand crab, its legs still flailing, in its beak. The bird's darting yellow eyes ward off any intruders.

Anne bends over the woman, bends her knees, and sinks slowly next to the sculpture, parallel to the figure, their arms running a similar length. Anne rests in the sand, gives her weight to the uneven surface. Her hands cup. They dig into the sand and drop it onto her legs and thighs and hips. She closes her eyes and feels the wet chill of undersurface sand. Her breathing disturbs the layer of sand that she has spread on herself, causes it to wrinkle, until she lies as still as possible, barely breathing. Reaching out as slowly as a growing flower, she touches the hand of the half-woman by her side and sleeps.

Thousands of wings ripple the air. Large, small. Unborn, undead, unseen guardians for the moment.

DAY THREE

He is leaning against the railing, the burlap bag resting at his feet. He wears the same red and black shirt of light wool and the black pants that shine like mirrors in places. Anne notices him as she walks down the ramp toward the pier in her cotton dress that is plaid with six buttons down the front.

Beneath them both, the tide is filling the basin, shortening the length of the piles, submerging the white barnacles on the pier's sturdy legs. They look at each other, then away at the rising water.

The dock fills with crabbers—Tongans with wives and children, baseball-capped seniors, tourists, a self-appointed overseer of novice crabbers who appears hungry and no older than nine years.

Anne is drawn to the man's back, even though there are many others leaning against the rail now, tossing large baskets on long ropes tied to the railing. She slides into the opening next to the man. She stands there, her hands on the wooden bar, looking first to the left at the disappearing shoreline, then to the right where the tide pours in at the channel's neck.

His shirt, she notices in peripheral vision, has been a feast for moths. His hair is dark and dusty, the comb tracks stiff. Yet he is not old, or finished.

The Tongans are pulling their baskets to the water's surface. The pincers of two large crabs are picking at the filet of rockfish tied to the wire-meshed bottom. Everyone gathers in a close circle, everyone except the man in the checkered shirt. Anne congratulates one Tongan who dangles a crab from the hooks of his large hand. She returns to her place at the railing.

The man bends over his burlap bag. He untwists its top and exchanges the empty can in his hand for a full one that reads Heidelberg Beer. When he puts his finger through the ring on the can's top, he half looks at Anne.

"Columbia River Valley," he says.

Anne looks at the tracking of veins on the back of her hand.

"Yup," he says and takes his first sip. "Columbia River Gorge country. I was a real Huck Finn, you know." He leans against the railing and picks at the lint on his sleeve. Anne leans to her left, away from him, to scratch under the strap of her sandal.

"I used to trap floating logs off the river and then nail them into a raft, lie on that raft on the river, naked for days in the sun." He wipes his mouth with the back of his hand and looks at Anne directly. "I've floated ever since."

Anne lifts both hands to the back of her neck and tosses her hair. She checks the ropes to see if anyone is pulling them in, if any crabs are riding out of the water. Then she looks down and sees flashes of reflected light from cans in the man's loosely woven burlap bag. The top of the bag has been twisted and untwisted many times. The weave of the bag is warped.

"You look Danish," Anne says.

"Could be," he says, staring into her eyes with eyes that seem to have absorbed all of the blues he has seen.

The young boy, overseer of crabs, wanders from catch to catch, issuing advice and instruction. He grabs the trapped crabs from the baskets as if he were lifting a hot frying pan from the stove.

"This one is a keeper," he says after he measures with a yellow plastic gauge. "It's wide enough between the points, and it's a male. See?"

After the catch has been tossed into a plastic bucket full of salt water, the boy crowds in between the man in the checkerboard shirt and Anne. "Aren't you gonna catch anything?" He shades his eyes as he looks up to them.

"I got my dinner." The man pulls a cob of corn from the inside of his shirt. It has been on someone else's plate, a smudge of mashed potatoes on one end, flecks of parsley scattered across the rows. He bites into the yellow kernels that have begun to cave in at the center. He is about her age, maybe halfway through his life. His eyes are incandescent, illuminating his desire to ramble, to keep possessions in a bag where he can tie a string around them and where they won't have a say. Smoke could curl out of those eyes, turn things to ashes if he stood still or made promises.

"What's in your bag?" Anne asks as the young boy runs off to the west side of the dock where a man in a cap that says "American Chemical" is having luck.

"This bag's my home," he says. "Anyone who likes my bag, well, she can come and live with me."

Anne follows after the boy to inspect the latest catch. The man in the cap wears eyeglasses spotted with seawater. Wringing his hands that are covered with brown blotches, he gloats over the plastic bucket where two crabs thrash in salt water.

"Change your water often," the boy is advising, "or they'll breathe in all the oxygen. They're poisonous when they die."

The man who looks like a Dane is behind her, close off her right shoulder. "Do you like my bag?"

Anne walks away, toward the Tongans who are pulling in a fresh catch. A small crab is escaping through the wire cage. Before it can be lifted from the trap, it has escaped and is skittering toward the pier's edge. It splashes into the bay, and Anne searches the tide that continues to pour through the narrow channel into the basin. Three boats bob in the neck of water, three boats with crab rings hanging from the sides.

Anne feels the man's eyes. She knows they follow her as she walks across the pier, back to the place by the railing, and then he's at her side again. "Do you want to know what's in here?" he asks.

"No," Anne says. "Excuse me for asking. Presumptuous."

He leans to the side and pulls a black wallet from his back pocket. It is chained to a belt loop. "Wanna see a picture? My son," he says as he presents a creased photograph. "He's five, but my wife didn't like my bag."

"Your son is handsome, like you, like my Danish uncles."

"You are, too." He wiggles the photograph back into the plastic keeper. A Swiss army knife is chained to the same chain as his wallet. "I've seen a lot, lady. Do you like my bag?"

"What do you mean?"

He twists the neck of his bag with both hands. No fire in the eyes now. They are clearer than the late afternoon light through a breaking wave. They promise nothing.

DAY FOUR

Anne watches a horse pound across the sand, its loose tail circling in the wind and speed. Its hooves pound across the chest of the woman in the sand, the woman who has been washed away except for remnants of her nose and cheeks. The nose is inverted now, pointing toward the center of the earth. The cheeks are spread into clumps of wet sand, a hoof print crushing one of them. The waves lick at the indentation. The horse skitters, dances, jumps away from the water that licks and swallows pictures in the sand. The print fills with water, a cup for a sandpiper. The sand shifts. Everything roars—the wind, the unsettled sea. Everything screams until it becomes silence and the wind wraps around the sand and falls.

Someone has left a doll on the beach. The doll has one arm over her head and one at her side. Australian crawl. Her hair swirls over her head like an ever-moving mass of tentacles. Bulbs of seawood lie scattered around her, bulbs to crack in two, slippery bulbs that shine and gleam out of the bed of brown weed nest. She lies there. No clothes, her hair tossed up away from her head, shiny blond seaweed.

Anne lifts the doll from the tangle, sand falling in delicate trickles to the beach as she wipes the doll's eyes, her back, her legs. She rearranges the hair and strokes the cheek.

The same little girl she saw before appears out of nowhere, her fists tight with indignance. "My doll. My doll." She grabs at the doll's hair, yanking until Anne's hand unfolds. "It's my doll."

"I'm sorry. I didn't know."

The girl doesn't cradle the doll or welcome her back home, but plunks her into the blue sand pail and carries her away on a swinging arm.

DAY FIVE

Anne follows a flock of sandpipers that trembles like gelatin when it runs from the waves. Anne follows the birds as they zigzag on their spider-thin legs from waves to shore and back.

Some stop to peck for sand crabs. Their reflections open and close like scissors. Some of them stand on one, some hop on two animated pencil lines. They scatter and gather. A perpetual game.

The figure of the sand woman is completely gone today, having bled her grains of sand into the water. Anne drags a stick in the sand as she walks to the point in the beach where she has full view of the pier jutting out over the water. No one can be distinguished at this distance, no single bodies, no particular shirt or black pants or burlap bags. Colors shift at the end of the pier, bodies cluster, then stretch out in varicolored threads, up and down the ramp. No way of knowing about the man.

The tide is returning to its patterns that it had left behind: crosshatched pen strokes, bird feathers, embedded wings. Thousands of wings in the mud, lying in patterns on the empty floor of wet sand. And Anne hears the wings behind her back where the ocean swells and contracts, the wings that beat the air. But she hears none in front of her. The sound is dampered by wet mud. The wings are spread to dry before they can rise again.

Birds on spider-toes and webbed feet pick and scratch in the mud that carries the impression of flight.

DAY SIX

Anne drives to the pier. The basin is covered with a shallow layer of water and rolling mounds of soft, watermarked mud. The tide is on its way out. No one stands at the railing waiting for a crab to walk into a trap. The crabs are riding the tide's pull from the shore.

Anne leans against the weathered wood of the railing and imagines the sleeve of a red and black shirt resting next to her bare arm. She remembers the vivid blue and wonders where the eyes have led the man. He may be walking north, along the highway. He may be sitting by an open fire. Maybe he has walked out with the tide. Anne looks up into the clear blue above and listens for the sound of wings.

The boy clomps down the wooden gangplank to the pier, rubbing the sleep from his eyes.

"I did the night tide."

"When does the tide come back in?" Anne asks.

"At 2:14," he says, bending over to look through the bars of the railing, surveying the map left behind by the tide.

"Where is your man?" the boy asks.

"What man?"

"The one who carries his lunch in his shirt."

"He isn't mine." Anne looks back at the row of cafes and tackle shops on the shore. No one in a checkerboard shirt leans against back entrances or searches through the trash. "He doesn't belong to anyone."

"I come here every tide," the boy says, "except I sleep through some of the night ones."

"Where do you live?"

The boy skips off to the west side of the dock to watch two seagulls fight over a scrap of food. Their white wings beat the air; they squawk as if their argument mattered.

"Maybe you should find that man," the boy says when he flits back to Anne.

"I have a home."

"No, you don't." The boy's eyes are large and deep black at center. Light reflects in them and dances across the pupils, quick to change, like butterfly wings. He cannot stand still in one place. His curiosity draws him to the cracks in the pier where he can spy on the tide pools and anemones with one eye.

"Do you live close by?" Anne asks, but the boy flaps his arms and runs across the wooden planks. Climbing through the bars of the railing, he scrambles over the edge onto an ancient wooden ladder at the edge of the pier.

Anne leans to watch his descent—thirty steps, some nailed crooked, some splintered in the middle.

"That's dangerous."

"Come on," the boy is yelling. "I wanna show you something. Hurry."

Anne looks back at the shore, the high places where the row of shops and restaurants is crowded with wandering tourists. She looks again for the red and black of a checkered shirt, searches each corner of the pier. Sometimes she thinks that it half fades into the light, a faint black, a pale red. Sometimes she hears his bag of aluminum cans rattle as he walks down the gangplank across the wooden boards. He is somewhere, but the air is half water and half wind and she can't trust the voices in the wind. Their whispers are indistinct. And the wings begin to beat the air again. The source of the wind. The locomotion for the rotation of the earth.

Anne bends from the waist. She sticks one foot through the railing, then the other. She squeezes between boards that splinter into the rough texture of her sweater, her back flat through the railing, barely clearing the space between boards. The ladder. Its steps are brittle, unsure. One step at a time, she climbs down, listening for the sound of cracking wood, listening to the wings beat around her head and ears.

She waves to the boy beneath her whose shout is slurred by the wind. And above her, with a halo of round sun framing his head, a man leans over and smiles, his eyes conduits for the sun behind his head. A shower of light falls on Anne as she squints to see if he wears red and black, but he is only a dark shadow.

Anne picks her way across languid pools that have not dried enough to leave patterns; she balances carefully on the tops of rocks and then the boy points to a half-sculpted woman and an empty Heidelberg can, together on the beach.

She shades her eyes and looks back up at the pier, dares the shadow to account for itself, but it, the man, is gone.

DAY SEVEN

She kneels, cupping large handfuls of damp sand. She pats it with the curve of her hands, smooths the grains into definition.

One part follows another—the shape of a cheekbone, cups to hold the eyes, the hair, the nose, a mouth. The lips are closed, rather than open for conversation. Now the neck, long and smooth, extra long, like the one Anne always wanted for herself. The shoulders. Anne bypasses the breasts and molds the waist, a slow, subtle curve rather than the indentation of an hourglass. The pelvis is a bowl for rice flowers, a basket for a baby, commodious, roomy, a center for conversation with the new. Using her fingernail, Anne traces a confusion of pubic hair. Swirls of a fingernail. Curling hair to blanket and protect the lips, the edge of a flower petal, a calla lily curving outward.

Arching her back, Anne sits tall, stretches her arms above her. Below her, the woman in the sand arches her back, then it falls to the sand. Not yet. And Anne spreads her hands, her fingers wide, versatile sculpting tools. The thighs. She shapes them as she would a loaf of bread, satin smooth as her mother had instructed when teaching loaves. Soft knees. The calves are rounded, no scars on the shins. No imperfections.

Anne bends over a foot, holds it close to her body, shelters it until the toes are formed, one, two, three, four, five. The heels, the arches. She kisses the feet, strokes her cheek against them.

Catching some of the wave that washes the beach next to her, she sprinkles her sculpture. A sheen of water on sand. The beginning of patina.

The breasts. Anne is tired. The waves are coming closer. Anne shapes one breast, coaxes it into a conic roundness, but she is tired. She drops her head to the unformed, planed side of the chest, cradles it, and drapes her arms around her creation.

And the wings float overhead, riding on an air current.